Jahamunite

M A O'Keefe

Published by Compass-Publishing UK 2021
ISBN 978-1-913713-78-2

Designed by The Book Refinery Ltd
www.thebookrefinery.com

1

Julia

Julia, daughter of Isabella and Jacob, had lived with her mother in the servants' quarters of Jahimian General Martinez, the leader of the King's army, all of her life; a pretty girl whose golden-brown hair and hazel eyes were in contrast to her mother's dark, almost black, hair and eyes of darkest brown. Julia's mother had told her that her father was a fine, honest and loyal soldier, who she reminded her of every day. He had died in battle days before Julia's birth and the General had taken pity on her mother and given his protection to them both.

By the time Julia was five years old she was proving to be a clever and inquisitive child. She would help her mother with the daily chores and was never happier than when out in the large garden digging weeds, laughing as she chased the birds away from newly planted seeds. As the years passed, she grew into a strong and healthy young girl. She was forever asking questions about her father and the life he and her mother had lived before his death. Some questions her mother would answer without hesitation, becoming misty-eyed and dreamy, as she recalled happier times. On one occasion, though, Julia asked the more pointed questions of who her father had been fighting against when he died, and if she had any other family.

Her mother breathed deeply and replied, "One day you will be ready for the answers to these questions, but for now you are too young to understand how such information could put you in danger. Your innocent chattering may put you in harm's way. Be certain, one day I will pass on to you all you need to know, but until that day we will live this life, keeping the roof over our heads and food in our stomachs, and blending into the very walls of this place to stay unnoticed."

Her mother's response left her shocked and confused but she resolved not to speak of these things again until she did understand. The one thing Julia was certain of was her mother's love; she knew this strange and unsettling response could only be for the best of reasons.

A few weeks before her sixteenth birthday, her mother came to her in the garden with a jug of cool water and some goblets. It had been an unusually warm start to spring, and they felt the touch of the sun upon their faces as they sat on the bench to drink. Isabella wrapped her arm around Julia, drawing her closer. Her hand made its way up to the back of her daughter's neck and touched the birthmark that lay hidden just below her hairline. This was something Isabella would do from time to time, almost as though she was checking it was still there. Isabella gasped. She lifted Julia's hair slightly to peek at the birthmark, which was shaped like a small island outlined by what looked like ripples of waves. Her eyes grew wide in alarm. Julia was taken aback.

"Whatever is the matter, Mamma?" she asked, in her confusion. "Do I have something growing on my neck? It feels very warm and tight. I thought the sun was warm as I worked but surely not hot enough to burn my skin."

Isabella dropped the hair back in place and looked around the garden, eyes darting here and there, to check if they were being watched.

"Mamma, what is it? What's wrong?"

Isabella looked at her. It felt to Julia as though her mother was searching the very depths of her soul.

"My darling, the time has come to answer all of your questions – but not here. We must be sure we cannot be overheard. This is something we cannot, must not, speak of to anyone – not even those who you think to be your closest friends."

Julia reached up and felt for the birthmark herself, surprised at the feel of it. "But, Mamma, it's twice its normal size! I feel it raised upon my skin like never before! Is it infected?"

Isabella quickly grabbed her daughter's hand and pulled it away. "No, my darling, not in the way you think. I will explain, but you must trust me and not speak of this or draw attention to it in any way. After we have served supper to the General and his family, we will have some time to ourselves. Simeon will remain in waiting for any requests the General may have, and you and I will talk while we clear the kitchen."

"Isabella! Isabella!" came a shout from the door of the kitchen.

It was Simeon, the General's right-hand man. He was tall and strong in stature, and the scar that ran down the left side of his face gave him an added look of brutishness. He enjoyed his power, always ready to dish out orders and prove that he outranked them. While his tongue often lashed out and made hurtful remarks, he had refrained from physically bullying them. Though Isabella knew the reason for this, her daughter did not. That particular secret was to be shared that very evening, along with others that would change the course of their lives forever. Isabella knew she must act quickly and put aside her fears. She must be strong and forceful, and leave Julia with no doubt as to what she must do, for her daughter's very existence depended upon it.

General Martinez had been joined at dinner by his wife and son, Marco, a bright twelve year old and the apple of both his father's and his mother's eye. Julia knocked over a goblet of wine while serving them. As she replaced it, she saw Marco grin at her in a friendly, reassuring way. He was a good-hearted person.

Simeon came into the room, bringing with him a fresh jug of wine.

"Get away to the kitchen, girl! You will go without supper for such waste!"

Marco appealed to his father. "Julia has worked in the garden, in the hot sun, all day. She is just tired, Father – and after all, it was only a goblet of wine."

Julia smiled at him, grateful for his support.

"Enough!" shouted the General. "Go to the kitchen, girl. Eat supper and off to bed with you! You can rise early and help your mother with the kitchen work in the morning – and take care to wear a hat out in the sun tomorrow."

Here, the General paused for a moment, then, looking Julia straight in the eye, in a deep and steady voice, he pronounced, "Too much sun can send you delirious."

"Thank you, sir," replied Julia and with that, made her way out of the dining hall.

Simeon's face left no doubt as to how livid he was. The curl of his lip, the blaze of fire in his eyes – Julia could be sure that he would have her pay for this when he was next left alone to wield his power.

Marco had winked at her as she left and it had taken all her control not to smile back, for this would surely increase Simeon's wrath.

Julia returned to the kitchen and found her mother laying their comparatively meagre meal before them.

"First, we shall eat," whispered Isabella. "Then, as the General has said, we can leave the kitchen till the morning and we will go to bed. There, I will tell you everything."

2

Truth

The mother and daughter lay facing each other on the small but adequate bed they shared.

Isabella began in hushed tones. "Your father, as I have told you many times, was a fine, handsome man and a loyal soldier. This is all true, but not in the way you have come to believe. Jahimia is all you've ever known and, of course, I am Jahimian-born, so how could you ever think anything other than that he was a soldier in the Jahimian army? But the truth, the real truth, is that he was not loyal to the Jahimians at all." She hesitated and took a deep breath. "Your father was Prince Jacob, the son of King Joalian of Hamunite!"

"What! I don't understand!" squealed Julia, creasing her forehead and shaking her head in disbelief.

"I know you don't understand, my darling, but there is much more to tell and I need you to be patient and listen carefully, for the story I pass on to you now holds the answers to so many of your questions. The Hamunites are believed to be protected by a charm of sorts that was bestowed upon their ruler many centuries ago. While most think this to be myth or a silly fairy story, I, as wife to the son of the King of Hamunite, know this to be true. The charm is recognised in the form of a birthmark. Only those born to become heir to the throne of Hamunite carry this mark."

Julia instinctively reached to feel her birthmark. "Do you mean what I think you do?" she asked, feeling her heart racing in her chest. "Are you saying that, in place of my father, I am heir to the King?"

"That is exactly what I'm saying. When your father died, his right to the throne of Hamunite was passed to his unborn child – the grandchild and rightful heir to the King. However, never before has the heir been female. So, even if there are some who believe that there is a living heir, they would not suspect that this person was a girl."

Isabella could see that her daughter's mind was spiralling. "My darling, there is still more that I must tell, which will most likely be even more difficult for you to hear. While you have always thought General Martinez to be our protector, he has, in fact, been our jailer!"

Isabella let the last word hang a moment before proceeding.

"Here, I must tell you things that will shock you and shake you to your very core, but you must listen and be strong, my darling, for your life and the eternal protection of the Hamunites depends upon what is to come."

Isabella went on. "In the heat of a summer's night, we lay sleeping in our small homestead in the land of Roscar. Your father had been banished from Hamunite by your grandfather, the King, for marrying me – a Jahimian whose race the Hamunites had been enemies with for many centuries. It is said that long ago Jahimia and Hamunite were one land and one people, known as Jahamunite. Civil war broke out amongst villages in the west and in the east. Many battles took place and many lives were lost on both sides. During one of the fiercest battles, the armies loyal to the lord of the western province of Jahamunite grew strong and many warriors from the east were slain. Among them was the son of King Heston, the rightful ruler of Jahamunite. In his despair and sorrow, Heston called upon the gods to bring the war and destruction to an end. Those who believe that there was once unity between these two lands talk of the biggest lightning bolt ever seen, smashing into the earth, dividing the land in two. What we now know as Hamunite became an island surrounded by tides ever turning and churning, sweeping relentlessly around the island. These conditions mean that it is impossible to enter Hamunite. Only the rightful ruler has the power to turn the tide and grant entry."

"I don't understand. If this is so, how did you and my father meet?" asked Julia, more and more astounded by what she was hearing.

"Though no one can enter, anyone can leave. Your father, my Jacob, left the island on a mission of peace. The King sent him to discuss terms of a peace treaty, thus showing his willingness to begin negotiations to bring the two lands together again. The population of Hamunite was diminishing due to a lack of girls being born over a period of many years. There was and still are too many men without wives and so it has become that more and more men have left in order to build lives and find themselves wives further afield. The men that come to the mainland of Jahimia try to make their way to Roscar, where they can be free to begin new lives. However, if they are caught by the Jahimian border patrols, they are imprisoned and tortured for any knowledge they may have of how Hamunite can be reached. The King took a gamble sending his only son here to Jahimia. He came to the very doors of the castle keep, here in Jahim

Town. Immediately, they knew him to be not only Hamunite, but someone of great importance – the light colour of his hair, his eyes a mixture of green with flecks of hazel…"

Isabella smiled to herself. She could see him clearly; the memory of his handsome face would remain with her always.

"The clasp on his cloak, bearing the Hamunite emblem of a beautiful woman with wings, known as a hawkwing messenger, identified him to be so. I was a member of the King's court and as soon as I laid eyes upon him, I knew he was special. As his eyes met mine, what passed between us in that moment was bewitchment. King Jared was at first pleased to welcome Jacob, though they were cautious when talking to each other not to make promises that would not be achievable. Although we cannot be certain, it is thought that if your father and I had not declared our love, the two lands would have formed a peace treaty, but the Kings of both lands disapproved of the match. We were being forced apart and so we ran away in the dead of night. We spent many weeks on the road dressed as farm labourers, travelling to villages, staying and working in the fields for a few days at a time until finally we passed into the land of Roscar, where we settled in a small cottage in the hamlet of Kriel. We were fortunate to find work with a man by the name of Tresgar Tremaine, who was to become our very dear friend and confidant."

"Why would they disapprove of you and Father being together? Surely the whole purpose of the mission was to bring the two lands back together? What better way could there be than a Jahimian marrying a Hamunite? Or were they hoping that Father would marry the other king's daughter?" Julia rambled on, trying to make sense of it all.

"Well, yes, it was something like that," Isabella hurriedly

replied. "Now, let me continue with my story for there is much to tell and time grows short...

"Not long after we settled there, I discovered I was having you and so Tresgar arranged for a holy man from the next valley to marry us. Some six months later, while we lay sleeping, exhausted from the day's work in the hot summer sun, they came. We were dragged from our bed. Your father fought like a lion. I screamed for help and struggled to free myself, but no help came. Our cottage was set alone on the outskirts of a small wood a mile or so away from the main farm and other dwellings. The cowards beat your father – one man against many – and when he could fight no more, he was struck down. He was struck down by the sword of General Martinez!"

Julia had been listening intently, tears coursing silently down her face, but now she gasped in horror and disbelief. "But ... but ... the General has given us a home and his protection! Why would he do such a thing?"

"My darling, the General does believe in the legend of the birthmark. In fact, he took me to his home and awaited your birth. When you were born, he knew straight away where to look for the birthmark, and although then it was barely more than a peculiarly shaped blemish, he knew! It is only because of this that you and I are still alive today. If the General realises that your birthmark is growing and changing at the rate it is, he will also realise that King Joalian is growing older and weaker. With this knowledge, he also knows that just before the King dies, the power of the turning of the tide will pass to you. This is why we must act quickly, before he suspects something. The people of Hamunite will send messengers in search of help. In search of you! The messengers are called hawkwings: small bird-like creatures with broad wings but human-like bodies. They will bring word of the King's condition and once the General knows this, he will take you from me. You will be under constant watch until the time is right for him to use you to cross the waters and on to Hamunite. Now, there is no time left to lose. We must make plans to get you out of here as soon as possible."

3

Escape

They had decided that she must make her escape there in the dead of night. It was sometime during Isabella's instructions that Julia realised her mother's intent to stay behind.

"I can buy you valuable time, my darling. I know it's been a lot to take in, but you really must understand the enormity of what your future holds and even more so, how your future will shape that of so many others."

Try as she might, Julia could not persuade her mother to go with her, so it was decided she would go by herself. Isabella promised that one day they would be together again.

"Know how much I love you, my darling daughter," she told her. "Carry my love with you in your heart and speak to me in your thoughts. Imagine me in conversation with you and answers will come to you. Destiny will guide you. Now, hurry and go. You must be far from here when the dawn breaks."

Julia made her way along the path that bordered the outside wall, through the vegetable garden, and climbed over the wicker fence. General Martinez's sprawling town house was built from Jahimian stone, with a wonderfully large garden that backed onto the edge of the town wall. The town itself sat upon the cliff face looking out to sea and the mysterious island of Hamunite. She stood now at the gates of the castle keep, through which the King of Jahimia himself resided. She found herself mindful that her own father had stood here to gain entry in the name of peace some seventeen years before.

But this was not to be her way out of the city, for she must not be seen. Instead, under the shadow of darkness, stealthily, she moved beneath bushes and behind abandoned market carts, making her way to the other end of town. Here, she came to the secret opening in the wall, one that she had discovered with Marco.

On an occasional day out of the house and grounds, they had run off ahead of Marco's tutor. They had hidden in an overgrowth of bushes which grew alongside the town wall; there, they had found an overturned wheelbarrow. What was under the barrow was ever so exciting. A shallow trench had been dug out of the earth, which led to a tunnel that burrowed under the town wall. Marco had mischief written all over his face.

"Let's do it!"

He grinned and before she knew it, he was gone – diving into the tunnel and wriggling his way into the outside world. She had followed him then and this was her route out now. However, on that day, they had sat on the hill in the sunshine, surveying the world before them.

This night was different. Her senses were sharp and the slightest rustle of the trees caused her body to tense. She made her way quickly through the tunnel and once outside the town walls, she stared down at the forest at the bottom of the hill. Whether the gods were looking down upon her or it was pure good luck she did not know, but the guards who patrolled the outer walls were nowhere to be seen. She ran down the hill and stumbled on a clump of earth, which sent her tumbling down to the bottom and smashing into an old oak tree.

Dazed and wincing from the pain caused by a bash to her head, she dragged herself up and made her way further into the forest. It was a slow and frightening process, so dark and extremely dense in places. She scratched her hands, face and legs on brambles. The scurrying, scratching, hooting and howling reminded her of the dangerous beasts that lived within the forest, such as the wild boar. Her heart thumped so wildly in her chest that she thought it would explode but still she kept on moving deeper and deeper into the forest.

Eventually, Julia noticed the forest beginning to thin out slightly and she came upon a stream, where she found droppings left by a wild boar that must have come to drink there. She took a drink herself and tried to wash some of her cuts and scratches. She knew the General would come after her, or if he would not come himself, he would certainly send some of his men, and with them, hounds to track her. She gathered together some of the boar droppings and rubbed them into a piece of sack cloth she had taken from the wood store in the garden, which she then wrapped around herself. As disgusting as it was, she hoped it would put the hounds off her scent and allow her time to rest up somewhere. She would need time to think and take in all that had happened. The decisions she had made thus far, as well as those still before her, must be the right ones; for if everything her mother had told her was true, the future of many depended upon her.

The stream was lit by the pale light of the moon, and it occurred to Julia that her best chance to confuse the trackers and enable her to put greater distance between them would be to walk in the stream itself. Despite the initial shock of the cold water around her ankles, Julia dared not go back onto land and leave footprints, and so she made her way on, cold and wet, step by step, through the remaining hours of the night.

As the morning sun began to rise, Julia judged that she had now put enough miles between herself and General Martinez to have earned a short rest. She stepped from the water and back onto the dry land, where she collected some leaves and brambles and lay down in a ditch, on the old sack cloth. She covered herself with more boar droppings and her findings from the forest floor. She felt the mark at the back of her neck and thought that it had not grown much larger. Perhaps the King of Hamunite was recovering, but even if this was so, she knew that she would not be able to turn back now. She hoped and prayed her mother was okay. In all her life, they had never been apart and now, as she lay on the hard, uneven ground, she had never before felt so alone. Finally, she gave way to great tiredness and slept.

Julia awoke to find the dappled light of day beginning to fade, as it forced its way between the branches of the trees, and was shocked that, in her exhaustion, she had slept for almost the entire day. She peered out from her hiding place; her stomach ravenous with hunger and her throat dry from thirst. The pain this caused her was nothing compared to the fear she had of being discovered. She dared not move until the sun had set and the cover of darkness had cloaked her once more.

As dusk began to approach, she knew she must make her move. How much time had passed since her mother's revelations? She could not be sure, but certainly half a night and the best part of a day. She tried to get up but her legs were numb. She rubbed them hard, grabbing her legs with her hands, forcing her knees to bend. Struggling onto all fours, she finally pulled herself upright. The small bag she carried contained dried bread, an apple and a small leather water carrier. She ate and drank a little. This revived her somewhat and she began to make her way to the outer region of the forest, where she would skirt its edge until she faced south. There, she would be able to see the Tovey Mountains in the distance. She must carry out her mother's plan to cross the Tovey River into the land of Roscar and make for the hamlet of Kriel. There, she was to look for the farmer, Tresgar, in the hope he would help her in her quest to reach Hamunite, when the time was right. It would take days, possibly weeks, to get there. She would find work on the farms as she travelled, just as her mother and father had done before she was born. Food and lodgings were all she would need to get by. The look of her hands would make her story believable – all that gardening had not been wasted.

Julia considered herself lucky to have got this far without any sign of being followed or coming across any wild creatures. As these thoughts flitted through her mind, out of the corner of her eye, she saw a rider on a grey horse appear from the forest, some way off. She drew back into the woodland, hid behind a chestnut tree and peered out. From behind the tree, she followed the rider's path with her eyes.

4

The Hunting Party

Julia was lucky that no one had yet come upon her, for General Martinez had indeed sent a small band of men, led by Simeon, to capture her and bring her back.

While Julia had been making her bed on the forest floor, back in the grand home of General Martinez, Isabella had made her way to the kitchen. It was early dawn and Simeon was already there waiting for her.

"Where's that little half-breed rat of yours?" he growled. "She's supposed to be here with you, earning her keep!"

Isabella kept her back to him and tried to keep her voice as normal as possible, as though it was just another day.

"Julia isn't well. It's as Marco said. She had too much sun and has been sick and feverish all night. She has only just fallen asleep. I can manage the work – her chores as well as my own. It will be fine. Honestly."

She managed to keep up the pretence throughout the morning. Marco had wanted to see Julia, but Isabella had told his mother that her illness could be catching and so he had been forbidden to see her.

When lunch had been served and consumed, and it came time for the servants to clear the dining table and clean out the kitchens, Julia was once again not on hand to tend to her duties. Simeon deemed that this had gone on beyond the point of ridiculousness and decided that he didn't care if she was sick or not, he wanted her put to work. He pushed past Isabella and made his way through the kitchens to their quarters. Isabella had packed the bed with clothes, but Simeon was not to be fooled. He was an experienced soldier, once a sergeant in the General's army. Others far wilier than Isabella had tried to trick him in the past, but he was not to be deceived. He tore the sheets away and without a further word, grabbed Isabella by the arm, dragging her through the house to the General's study. Pushing open the door, he threw her onto the floor. The General looked startled.

"What is the meaning of this? How dare you burst into my office in such a manner?" demanded Martinez. "One day, Simeon, you will go too far. What is the problem now?"

A sneer appeared on Simeon's face. "The daughter, she's gone."

"Gone? Gone where?" asked the General.

"Run away. She's disappeared and who knows how long this conniving madam's been lying," he said, nodding towards Isabella. "The bed was packed out with clothes. As if I would fall for that old trick!"

The General rushed around the table and dragged Isabella to her feet. Gripping her arms, he shouted in her face, "Where is she? Where has she gone?"

Then, it dawned on him. His face took on a look of excitement that quickly turned to anger. "It's started, hasn't it?"

"She's gone, and you won't find her. It's her destiny, General, not yours." Isabella stared at him defiantly.

General Martinez raised his hand high before bringing it down and striking Isabella with such force she fell to the stone floor, banging her head. She sank into a state of unconsciousness.

"Go to the garrison up at the keep! Select half a dozen men to follow you and track her down! Use the hounds. We'll have her back in no time and then we shall see. Oh yes, Isabella, we shall see whose destiny will be fulfilled."

"As you wish, General. I will depart as soon as possible. What about the mother?" Simeon asked.

"Throw her on her bed. She'll be fine. Put her under guard, though. I may still need her as a bargaining tool."

Looking Simeon directly in the face, he said, "And Simeon, time is of the essence here. We have no knowledge of how close the changeover may be. I want her back in one piece. Do NOT let me down!"

Simeon assembled a band of six soldiers who he knew to have the kind of character he needed – men who were strong and forceful, yet would take orders without question. They would have to follow his lead at every turn without asking questions about the importance of this mission. For as loyal as they were, if they knew or suspected the power the girl could wield, there remained a chance they could break ranks.

They set out in pursuit of their quarry in the knowledge that although Julia had a considerable head start on them, they were on horseback and would be able to cover the ground at greater speed. By late afternoon, they had tracked her to the stream, just as she had suspected they would. Julia's intuition that the hounds would be put off by the scent of the boar droppings had proven correct and from there, Simeon no longer had guaranteed knowledge of which way she had headed. He tried to analyse what Julia would do. He did not credit her with much sense and thought that once she was out of the castle walls, she would make for the quickest route to the coastline closest to Hamunite, and so he led the men upstream. They ventured northeast, unaware that Julia had actually gone southwest. The fact that the hounds had lost the scent bothered him, but he could only assume she had kept to the stream. In this, he was indeed correct, but he was far too arrogant to think that she would take any option other than the easiest route to Hamunite.

Unbeknownst to Simeon, high up in the trees, someone was watching the hunting party, undetected. A slight twitch came to the observer's lips. It could almost have been a smile.

Julia felt glad of her good fortune thus far. She knew that she must make her way to one of the farm dwellings that lay close by in order to find shelter for the night. The rider was so far ahead of her now he would not see her; dusk was giving way to night.

"What you looking at?"

A voice from behind made her jump. She turned to see what seemed to be a child, though the voice belonged to someone much older, covered in a hooded cloak made from sack cloth. The hooded figure tilted its head from left to right, weighing her up.

"I'm ... err ... I'm just looking ... looking at the view," Julia stuttered. "Though, never mind me, who are you and what are you up to, sneaking up on people like that?" she said, gathering her composure.

"Well, first of all, I didn't just sneak up on you. I have, in fact, followed you through the woods and watched over you while you slept. A good job I did, too, otherwise the boars would have joined you in your bed, young lady, smelling the way you do. Second of all," and here the creature pulled back the hood, "your mother sent me to watch over you!"

"Mikel!" Julia exclaimed in surprise. "But I don't understand. Why ever would my mother ask you to watch over me?"

Mikel was known to Julia as the kindly dwarf who came to the kitchen door each day to deliver the milk. If Simeon wasn't around, some days he would stop and chat, always asking after the mother's and daughter's health. Only now did Julia realise the significance of what had seemed to her like mere small talk. Each day Mikel would ask, *How are you both today?* and her mother would routinely reply, *We're fine, Mikel. Should that change, you'll be the first to know*. Although part of their everyday conversation, this was a very strange thing to say to a dwarf who delivered the milk.

"Nothing is ever what it seems, my dear. After the secrets that have been revealed to you recently, you of all people should know that. I went to the house early this morning, as usual, and your mother was waiting for me. She had managed to successfully keep your leaving a secret and dispatched me at once to find you. Oh, and by the way, I don't think the rider on the grey horse is anything to worry about."

With that, he set out across the fields with Julia following him.

5

Revelations and Mysteries

Julia and Mikel made their way downhill across farmers' fields, being careful to keep to the edge so as not to ruin the crops, till they came upon a cluster of farm dwellings and barns. It was dark by now and lamps were lit in some of the windows of the main farmhouse. They knocked at the door. An elderly woman opened, small in stature with greying hair escaping from a cotton bonnet. She seemed to straighten up, as if to give an air of authority.

"What is it you're wanting, knocking me door at this late hour?!"

"We know it is late, ma'am, and we apologise for calling at such an hour, but my friend and I have been travelling for some time and are desperate for somewhere to rest for the night," pleaded Mikel in the politest of manners.

"Well, who are you and where you travellin' to?" asked the woman.

Julia had just opened her mouth to speak when Mikel trod on her foot and quickly began.

"We belong to the circus and are heading out to join up with them. I have been ill and the girl here is the daughter of one of the other performers. She was left behind to care for me."

"Oh, circus folk, are you? Well, I ain't got nothin' against you travellin' folk. At least you're workin' for a living."

She bent forward, holding her apron to her mouth, and looked at him suspiciously.

"This illness, it wasn't anythin' that was catchin', was it?"

"No, no, nothing like that. I had an accident that left me with a broken leg, but it's all mended now. All fine. We're off to join up with the others again, as I said."

"Well, all right then. You can sleep in the barn and if you've got money, I'll sell you some bread, cheese and milk. Oh, and I don't know what it is that you smell of, young lady, but a good wash wouldn't go amiss. I've got an old dress you can have for a few extra coins while you wash yours, or maybe get rid of it if you can't get that smell out," she said, wrinkling her nose.

Julia acknowledged the old woman's offer. "Thank you. You are very kind."

With Julia cleaned up, and they both having eaten, they finally settled down for the night in the barn across the yard from the house. Julia was so very tired but she knew that she would never sleep with so many questions left unanswered.

"Mikel, how on earth did you come up with such a story?"

"Well, it's more of a truth than a story. Just that it happened quite some time ago and you're not the girl who looked after me – that was your mother."

Julia looked at him in astonishment.

"My mother looked after you! When? When was this?"

"Well, some twenty or so years ago. I was not much more than a boy myself and Isabella, a young girl, maybe around a year younger than you are now."

Julia was intrigued by what Mikel could tell her.

"Please go on. I know so little of my mother's past and what I do know has been distorted or fabricated to hide the truth from me. Although I know this to be with good reason, I am eager to hear all you can tell me."

"Very well. I shall tell you how your mother and I became such good friends and why I am here to help you. I was born into the circus; my father was a tumbler and rather challenged in the height department, much like myself. My mother, a beautiful, graceful woman, who was a foot or so taller than my father, was a trapeze artist and amazed the crowds with her daring acrobatics. As I grew up, I too became skilled at both tumbling and flying from swing to swing upon the high trapeze. Hence, while others are tracking you on the ground, my skills on the trapeze have equipped me well to move quickly through the trees of the forest and to observe what is happening far below on the forest floor."

"You have seen someone following me then?" asked Julia.

"Yes, I have, but they are no longer on your trail. We should be able to rest peacefully tonight. However, we must not become complacent; we will need to set out early in the morning. Now, back to my story or we will never get any sleep tonight."

"But who was it? Was it anyone you know?" Julia was suddenly too concerned with the threat of any imminent danger to hear more of Mikel's story.

The dwarf sighed. "It was Simeon with a small band of men from the King's army, but he has travelled northeast, whereas you and I go south west, so there is a good distance between us. He will mistakenly believe you to be naive enough to make the quickest route to Hamunite. His arrogance will not allow him to credit you or your mother with the foresight to make a real plan. Now, do you want to hear the story of our friendship or not?"

"Yes, yes, please go on," Julia pleaded reassuringly, though she couldn't help feeling troubled knowing it was Simeon who had been sent to look for her. She hoped above all else her mother was safe.

Mikel resumed his tale. "In my fifteenth year, we travelled back to the small town of Triorey. Its lord lived in a beautiful manor house at the edge of the town, which backed onto farmland. He owned all the land around for miles and the farms surrounding the town were worked by tenant farmers, meaning the circus would always have to gain the lord's permission before setting up. Lord Alessandra was always happy enough for us to return year after year. He saw it as a social event for the farm workers and townsfolk. This particular year, we had set up in the field a mile or so away from the manor house. I was part of both my parents' acts and whilst performing on the high trapeze, I had a fall. My leg was broken below the knee. I was taken to the manor house, where a doctor came and after administering chloroform, set my leg in a splint and told me I would need to rest for some months. Your mother and I had known each other since we were children. Of course, we were of different social standing and had her father realised the friendship we had developed over the years, he would not have approved. Your grandmother, Lady Alessandra, however—"

"Whoa! Hold on a minute!" Julia interrupted. "My grandparents were Lord and Lady Alessandra?!"

"Well, yes. Sorry, I keep forgetting you know so little of your family's past," Mikel apologised.

"So, I am the granddaughter of a lord and lady!" Julia said this as a statement, as if voicing it out loud would make it seem less incredible. "Okay, I believe you, but this being so, how on earth did you and Mamma end up in Jahim Town with her being part of the royal household?"

"Now, you just hold on a minute, I'm getting to that. Lady Alessandra knew Isabella and I had a childhood friendship and when Isabella pleaded for me to be allowed to stay and rest in the servants' quarters at the manor, being the kind and caring woman she was, your grandmother arranged my stay there, initially to do light duties in the kitchen. Being young and well looked after, my recovery was complete within six months, but almost five years on I was still at the manor, although my duties had become much more varied. I was a trusted and loyal employee, certainly to Lady Alessandra and your mother. My relationship with your grandfather was rather more formal. I knew my place when he was around."

Mikel said this with a certain air of wistfulness.

"My own parents returned year after year and tried to persuade me to go with them, but I felt I had a duty to Isabella, as though somehow our destinies were entwined. So it was that when her father took her to the King's court in Jahim, but then returned to Triorey alone, I couldn't understand why. Your grandmother seemed very agitated and the following day, when Lord Alessandra went out riding, she called me to her sitting room. Her revelations left me reeling."

Mikel shook his head as if what he was about to say was still something he couldn't quite believe could happen.

"King Jared of Jahimia was widowed when his first wife gave birth to a daughter, Jasmina. Jasmina is the same age as your mother and it was at first thought that Isabella would be a good companion for Jasmina. The King had never thought to remarry, until that is that he set eyes upon Isabella. Suddenly, his reason for Isabella to become part of the court changed and he bargained with your grandfather for her hand in marriage."

"What? You must be joking?" blurted Julia in astonishment.

"No, young lady, I'm not joking. Now, you need to be quiet and listen as it is very late now and soon we shall need to sleep. So, let me fill you in quickly on the rest of this story. Lord Alessandra tried to persuade the King otherwise but he was having none of it. He sent Lord Alessandra home under the threat of his land and property being taken over by the military. He was told to return within the month whereby he would see, once Isabella had got to know the King better, that she had become a willing bride. Lady Alessandra dispatched me at once, under orders to keep the fact that I knew Isabella a secret. She set up a meeting for me with a local dairy farmer, who took me on to help with deliveries. Of course, this was my way into the castle keep. I hadn't been there more than two days when Jacob arrived. He had been sent on a mission of sorts by his father, King Joalian of Hamunite."

"Yes, yes, Mamma told me all about that," said Julia, rather impatiently. "So, this is why the treaty fell apart. My father ran away with my mother, the woman King Jared intended to marry. But I still don't quite understand why my grandfather banished them from Hamunite."

"Well, I took them to the coast town of Great Holm, where Jacob's ship was anchored. They made their escape and Jacob sent word to his father, the King, by a hawkwing messenger. The messenger hawk reported Jacob's homecoming to the King.

Looking out from the tower of his fortified home onto the sea as the ship approached, he turned the tide to allow them to enter the Hamunite harbour. When the King discovered what Jacob had done, in his temper at the damage done to any chance of a treaty, he banished the young lovers from Hamunite there and then. They sailed off in a small fishing boat back to Jahimia in order to travel in disguise to Roscar."

Mikel sighed. "Now, young lady, we must sleep. The dawn will be upon us soon and we need to travel some distance over the next few days. There will be plenty of time for you to learn more as we travel."

"Goodnight, Mikel," Julia yawned. Although her head was full with so much to try and make sense of, before long she fell into a disturbed sleep.

6

Leonal

While Julia had been making her way through the woods on the night of her escape, in the coast town of Great Holm, some ten miles or so from Jahim Town, a young man by the name of Leonal was deciding what he should do. His bedridden father had passed away a few nights before, after much suffering. Captain Jules Mathius had been a strong and brave captain in the King's army who, when leading a small group of men on a border patrol, was badly injured in a fight with a band of lawless rebels known as Bondsmen, named after their leader, Macki Bond. Captain Mathius had been left paralysed by his injuries. He had been a difficult and depressed patient for his wife, Maria, and their son, Leonal, who had taken on any kind of work available to them to ensure they'd survive, and had existed in this way for the last five years.

Once a well-respected leader, Jules found it difficult to come to terms with having everything done for him. Having to watch his beautiful wife and son work like slaves to keep a roof over their heads and food in their bellies had been hard to bear. The only time he seemed to come to life was when he recounted his stories from his past glories as a soldier. Leonal, now seventeen, had listened avidly to these stories from the age of twelve. He felt this was his only link to the true man he knew his father to be.

When Jules told these stories, he often spoke of his good and loyal friend Tresgar. Some years older than Jules and his superior in those days, Tresgar had taught Jules all he knew, passing on the skills that had enabled him to rise up through the ranks. Tresgar himself left the service of the King after he was injured, a few years before Leonal was born, and had returned to his family home in the land of Roscar.

Although he had fully recovered, Tresgar had decided that farming life was where his future lay. However, he had still returned to Jahimia on a number of occasions since then and when he did, he always made sure to call at the Mathius family home.

When Jules was first paralysed, Tresgar had come to offer his assistance and had helped the family secure a small cottage on the edge of town. The home they had lived in all of Leonal's life was an army quarters, owned by the King, and was to become the home of the new Captain of the Guard of Great Holm. A few weeks before, when Tresgar had last visited, the friends had shut themselves away in Jules' room for a private discussion.

Now, Leonal dwelled upon that final meeting between the two men and what his father had told him hours before his death.

"Things are changing, Leonal. Tresgar knows the future of Jahimia is changing. I want you to go to him. Go to his home in Roscar. There is much you can learn from him. I know I'm not long for this world, my son, but you must not dwell on this; it is time for me to go. I only wish it could be me who was seeing you pass from boyhood into manhood. You see me lying here and you think you know the reason for how I came to be this way. Things are not always what they seem, my boy. Take heed of what Tresgar tells you for he is a wise and caring man."

Jules began to cough and splutter. Leonal quickly poured a goblet of water and, supporting his father, held it to his lips to drink. When Jules lay back down, his breathing became more staid. He closed his eyes and bade Leonal leave him rest. As Leonal made to go from the room, his father called to him in a quiet, rasping voice.

"Leonal, take care of yourself and your mother and promise me you will join Tresgar in Roscar."

Leonal stood with his hand on the doorknob and turned to look at his father. He could see how weak he was and realised that there was nothing to be gained by arguing and so he made a promise to his father to go to Roscar and to live and work with Tresgar on his farm. There, he would learn how to use a sword, how to track and how to become a man who could take care of himself and others.

Leonal's thoughts turned to his mother, who had insisted she would be fine staying in the cottage. She explained that the work she did mending the great fishing nets would mean they could keep the cottage and that she would have her friends, the other women who worked alongside her, to keep her company.

"The cottage is our home now and you will come home one day when you are ready. I shall be here waiting for you, my son. Tresgar looks on you as one of his own family; he will take good care of you. It is what your father wanted," Maria stated.

"I think I already know how to look after myself," Leonal

argued. "I already handle a sword well. And how did my father think I managed to bring home extra meat for the table? Did he not know how good a tracker and an archer I am? And part of my promise was to take care of you. How am I to do that in Roscar?"

Maria looked at her tall, handsome son, not yet a man but no longer a boy. He had had to grow up quickly. He had become physically strong from all the hard work. Typically Jahimian in looks, his dark hair flopped across his forehead and his eyes of ebony burned with intensity, as he struggled to come to terms with leaving her and carrying out the promise to his father. She needed to make this as easy for him as possible, though it would break her heart to see him go. And so she tried to appease him by answering his questions with reasoning.

"Of course he did, but as he explained to you, his reasons for sending you to Tresgar are nothing to do with putting food on the table. Your father told you Jahimia is on the brink of change, although I have no understanding of what he meant by this. I know he would not ask you to do this unless he was sure it was the right thing to do. Changes are coming. Tresgar knows of things that will happen and he is a good man who will follow the right path. You are destined to follow him on that path for, if what Tresgar told your father is true, good men will need to stand up and be counted on for the sake of many."

And so Leonal decided if for no other reason than to satisfy his curiosity, he would travel to Roscar to the home of Tresgar and discover what the changes that seemed so intriguing could be.

With a heavy heart at leaving his mother behind, he set out the next day. Tresgar, as generous as ever, had on that final visit left behind a beautiful grey mare.

"You will be in need of a good horse – and you will soon repay me when you come and work with me and my family on the farm," Tresgar said, as he tried to persuade Leonal to accept his gift.

As Leonal made his way through the forest, heading towards the Tovey Mountains, he was alerted to the sound of barking hounds. He wondered who could be hunting in the forest and knew to be careful, for ruthless characters could be found around these parts. Before he knew it, he was surrounded by soldiers.

"What have we got here then?" their leader sneered at Leonal, dismounting his horse and catching hold of the reins of the grey mare.

As he came alongside horse and rider, Leonal noticed a fierce-looking scar across the man's left cheek.

The man fixed his eyes upon Leonal in an intimidating manner and resumed his questioning. "What are you doing out here on your own, boy? Don't you know the dangers of travelling alone in these woods? Why, if the wild boars don't get you, there are always the Bondsmen; they'll slice you in two soon as they look at you."

"I know only too well what the Bondsmen are capable of."

Taking in the Guardsmen's uniforms, Leonal decided this was a time when using his father's name could offer him a way out of a potentially bad situation. "I am the son of Captain Jules Mathius. I am sure you will have heard of him and will understand my own hatred of the renegade Bondsmen."

The tone of the Guardsmen's leader did indeed change upon hearing this information. "The son of Jules Mathius? Is that so?" he said. "I am Simeon Emires, Lieutenant to General Martinez himself. I do indeed know of your father."

Although he had not fought alongside Jules directly, Simeon knew and respected him as a soldier and this immediately made him look at the boy in a different light.

"Where is it that you're off to? Could you be ready to join the Guardsmen and follow in your father's footsteps? Not that Captain Mathius has been able to make any footsteps in recent years due to those damn Bondsmen low lives. You would do well to avenge him in this way, I think."

Simeon went on, without waiting for answers to the questions he'd posed. "Anyway, enough of this. I have other, more pressing, matters at hand. I guess then you have journeyed from Great Holm. Have you passed by a girl – mixed blood with Hamunite features?"

"No, I have come across no one until now and this meeting with you, sir," Leonal answered politely.

He thought he knew the type of man Simeon would be; bitterness for some past misfortune hung around him and the slightest provocation would give him an excuse to cause pain to others. No, he must be wary of this man.

"Well, we must be on our way, boy. You get yourself off to Jahim Town and they will welcome you into the castle keep, of that I am sure."

With that, Simeon remounted his horse and was gone, with his band of men following close behind.

Leonal pushed on through the forest for he had no intention

of going to Jahim Town. For some reason he could not quite place, he knew it would not be advisable to tell Simeon where he was headed. Intuitively, he felt it best to keep where he was going to himself. So it was that Leonal headed south and out through the forest towards the Tovey Mountains. Unknown to him, he was being watched by a young girl and a dwarf, tucked away high in the treetops.

7

Misunderstandings

Leonal followed a trail that ventured around the other side of the field that Julia and Mikel had passed through, coming out on the other side of the farm, where the farmer was herding cows back to their field below after milking.

"Where you off to, young man? Not travelling too far at this time of evening, I hope? It'll be dark soon and some unsavoury types can be found hanging around these parts."

"Thank you for your concern, sir, but I was hoping you might allow me to bed down in one of your fields for the night. I have all I need except for water for myself and my horse. Does the stream from the forest venture this far?" asked Leonal.

"Aye boy, it does. Comes out other side of the farm buildings, but you be welcome to use the barn for the night and in return you could do me a good turn and help me get these cows to bottom field over there," he said, pointing to a field in the distance.

"Sounds like a bargain to me," replied Leonal with a friendly grin.

The farmer was unaware that his wife had already allowed Julia and Mikel to sleep in the barn. It was shortly after they had fallen asleep that he and Leonal arrived in the farmyard.

Julia slept fitfully, but the clip clop of horses' hooves ringing out on the farmyard stone floor woke Mikel immediately. He heard the murmuring of voices and sneaked up to the hayloft above the barn. Peering out through a small crack in the hayloft door, he could see the boy watching the farmer and his wife talking in hushed voices but gesticulating to each other, obviously at loggerheads. Finally, the old couple went inside the farmhouse and the boy made his way over to the barn.

The door to the barn squeaked open and the boy entered slowly, bringing his horse with him. He whispered into the darkness of the barn, "Hello, are you awake?"

With the barn door now ajar, a ray of moonlight shone into the corner, where something shifted slightly. Leonal, unnerved by the farmer's talk of unsavoury characters and also thinking back to the meeting in the forest with the Guardsmen, moved his hand to the horse's flank, where his father's sword lay sheathed. A rustling noise alerted him to something coming up behind him but before he could turn around, Mikel, swinging swiftly from the rafters, landed on Leonal's back and placed a dagger at the boy's throat.

"Some quick and honest answers are needed, boy, otherwise this dagger will do its job. Do we understand each other?" Mikel whispered in a menacing voice.

By this time, the disturbance had woken Julia from her sleep. She screamed Mikel's name in fright.

"Nothing to worry about, girl," snapped Mikel. "I have it all under control. We have company and I'm just about to find out who this young man is and why he might be following us."

Conscious of the dagger at his throat, Leonal thought it better he cooperate, at least for the moment. "My name is Leonal and I can assure you I am not following you or anyone else. I am just travelling through and stopped to help the farmer and take up his kind offer of a night's rest in his barn."

"Okay – where have you travelled from and where are you going to?"

"I have left my home in the harbour town of Great Holm and am heading south to Roscar to take up work there," answered Leonal.

"Mikel, I think the boy tells the truth," said Julia.

"Oh, you do, do you? Since when did you gain the experience to know such things?"

"It's just a feeling, that's all. I don't know how else to explain it," replied Julia softly.

"She has good instincts. Please listen to her!" begged Leonal.

Mikel loosened his grip on Leonal and jumped down from his back.

"Thank you," said Leonal.

Julia, now stood up, slowly came forward. Leonal could not quite see her face in the small amount of light generated by the moon. All he could think of was how to get out of the situation he had found himself in.

"I can see you don't really want to share the barn, so I can just be on my way. No problem. No problem at all. You just want to keep the girl safe, that's all. I perfectly understand."

"I think you should stay and share the barn for the night. If what you have told me is honest and true, you have nothing to fear and we have nothing to worry about concerning you. Am I right?" quizzed Mikel.

"Yes, yes, that is true," answered Leonal.

"Right, you sleep over there. There's a stable holding perfect for you and your horse," Mikel directed, pointing to the opposite corner of the barn. "Oh, but just in case, I'll look after that sword of yours," he added.

Leonal hesitated for a second but then decided it would be easier to give in gracefully. He just hoped they were as honest as he was. It occurred to him that the softly spoken girl could be the one the Guardsmen were looking for. Was this the mixed-blood girl Simeon had spoken of? He could not see her features and colouring in this light and anyway, he certainly didn't want to get involved in anything to do with the scar-faced lieutenant. The thought of a young girl at the mercy of such a brute gave him an uneasy feeling, but he could not be distracted; he was going to see Tresgar and that was that.

And so it was that the travellers, as wary as they were weary, settled down for the night. Mikel placed himself strategically between the boy and Julia, and when he was sure he could hear the boy breathing the soft rhythmical breaths that come with deep sleep, Mikel finally allowed himself to fall into a light slumber.

8

The Search

After leaving Leonal, Simeon and his men headed north to Great Holm. Emerging from the forest, they could see the coastal town some way off in the distance and raced on towards it. As they got closer, they slowed their mounts to a trot since the approach into Great Holm was on a steep camber and was made by following a zig-zagging trail. On their descent they came across a local dairyman with a cart, making his way out of the town. Simeon promptly stopped him.

"You there! We're looking for a girl," he began.

"Oh right. Could do with one of them myself," the man chortled, interrupting the lieutenant.

"This is no laughing matter, you fool. This girl is a runaway; a mixed-blood Hamunite. She is from the household of General Martinez and is to be returned for her own good," snarled Simeon.

The man in the cart looked directly into Simeon's eyes and enquired coolly, "She stolen somethin' of worth has she or done somethin' real bad? I'm thinkin' she must've to warrant a band of Guardsmen searchin' for her."

"Never you mind what she's done – that's no business of yours!"

"Well, no, it's not, but if there's a reward to be had, I'll be sure to keep an eye out for her."

"No one has spoken of any reward. Now, on your way and should you come across such a girl you would do well to pass the information on to me immediately. You can leave any messages at the General's town house."

With that, Simeon cracked his whip down on the flank of the carthorse. Startled, it charged off; the driver hanging onto the reins for all he was worth. Simeon and his men galloped on, sniggering at the driver's difficulty to bring the horse under control. They would not have thought it so funny if they had known who the dairyman would show his allegiance to.

Simeon and his men went on into the town and down to the harbour, where the women worked along the wall drying and repairing fishing nets. They questioned the women, one of whom happened to be Maria, Leonal's mother. As they had not seen anyone they could offer no assistance, but their curiosity was aroused by such a search for someone who should be of no real importance. Simeon and the men went on to search any boats that had been moored in the harbour and they questioned the fishermen about boats or ships that had recently set sail with passengers on board.

Finally, Simeon called at the town house of the Captain of the Guard of Great Holm. He notified him of the situation at hand, without telling him the real reason the girl was wanted so urgently. After a meal at the invitation of the Captain, Simeon and his men set off once more, this time back to the house of General Martinez in order to interrogate Isabella. *I'll get some answers from that madam or she'll be sorry*, he thought to himself. Oh yes, he'd enjoy making her talk; that he was sure of.

The dairy farmer had barely slowed his pace. Once out of sight of the Guardsmen, he regained control of the carthorse but rode her as hard as he might dare. Upon reaching home, he hurriedly climbed from his cart and darted into the farmhouse. He ran up the stairs and into the bedroom, where he flung the shutters wide open. He then closed his eyes and summoned the messenger.

Moments later he heard her voice inside his head, announcing that she had come. He opened his eyes and saw the hawkwing gliding effortlessly towards him before landing on the window ledge. She stood no more than fifty centimetres in height. Her body had a human form; however, instead of skin, she was covered in beautiful plumage.

Hawkwings' faces were of outstanding beauty, with large eyes outlined by long, dark lashes. This, combined with their graceful and lithe limbs, made them a sight to behold. One of the rarest of species, the hawkwings were native only to Hamunite and would not nest or reproduce anywhere else in the world. It was said that hawkwings were created specially to carry messages for the gods. This being the case, a hawkwing could only be summoned telepathically and would only appear if the message was one of importance to the protection of the island of Hamunite.

Without uttering a word, the farmer passed the message from his mind to that of the hawkwing and within seconds, off it flew without a sound. He watched it disappear across the horizon, thankful for his encounter with the brutish, scarred soldier. Very soon, word of the search for Julia would reach Lady Alessandra.

9

Discoveries

Mikel was the first to wake. In turn, he gently shook Julia. When she opened her eyes, he put a finger to his lips; a warning to stay quiet. He bent to whisper in her ear, "Let's get out of here before the boy wakes up."

Julia looked across to where Leonal lay sleeping. She hesitated for just a second but then looked at Mikel, nodded in agreement and as quietly as they could, they packed their belongings. Before departing, Mikel lay the boy's sword down by his side, prompting Julia to smile warmly at the dwarf. They crept from the barn out into the farmyard and started along the track towards the Tovey Mountains. From there, they would follow the river on to Roscar.

Leonal had been awake. He listened to the pair, as they had tried to sneak out unheard. He decided to keep up the pretence of being asleep; he certainly had no wish to make small talk with them. The dwarf was jumpier than a bag of frogs, but what if the girl was the one who the Guardsmen were looking for? Should he say something? His indecision was causing him to become annoyed with himself. These people meant nothing to him and they, or at least the dwarf, had been very aggressive. Why should he worry? There again, the dwarf had left his father's sword. No, decided Leonal; it was best to stay out of that whole mess.

Soon after Mikel and Julia left, Leonal began to make ready to move out himself. As he and his horse entered the farmyard, the farmer came out of his house and beckoned to Leonal.

"Good mornin', young man. How about a little more help for an old fella? In return, the missus will make you a hearty breakfast to set you on your way."

A grin broke out on Leonal's face. True enough he was hungry. Why not, he thought.

"What is it you want me to do then?" he asked.

"Oh, nothin' too hard – help get the cows back in for milkin' and maybe chop a few logs for the missus. Them strong young arms of yours will get the job done in half the time I could."

"Go on then," grinned Leonal. "Sounds like a bargain if the breakfast is as hearty as you say."

Leonal and the farmer went to begin their work and thoughts of the girl and the dwarf began to drift from the young man's mind.

Back in Jahim Town, Simeon and his men had returned to relay the details of their search to General Martinez. The General was not at all pleased with the outcome so far and had sent for Isabella, who had been kept under guard since the discovery of Julia's disappearance.

The guard pushed Isabella roughly into the General's study, where Martinez was seated behind his desk. Simeon was stood to his right-hand side. He glared at Isabella.

"Where have you sent Julia?" asked the General.

Isabella looked him straight in the eye; the cut and bruising on her forehead, a reminder of the rough treatment she had received, did nothing to diminish the challenging stare she gave him now as she answered his question.

"I do not know where she is and even if I did, I would have no intention of telling you!"

"Obviously you don't know exactly where she is at this moment, but you do know where she is heading – and you will tell me, Isabella," spoke the General in a calm but commanding voice.

Isabella said nothing; she just stared at the General.

"Give me an hour alone with her. I'll soon get some information," snarled Simeon.

"Maybe we will have to resort to that eventually, Simeon, but for the moment I'm thinking back to this lady's past and her family home in Triorey. Her father is dead, of course. A heart attack after losing his lands, they say; a suitable punishment for this madam running off with the Hamunite."

All the while he was speaking, General Martinez never took his eyes from Isabella's face. Watching for any trace of a reaction, he spoke on.

"There is still the mother, however. Lady Alessandra remains living in the family home. Of course, it's a dilapidated wreck now due to the lack of income. The farms and surrounding land were taken by the King in his anger at their daughter's traitorous ways."

Still, Isabella showed no sign or emotion.

"Maybe you should pay Lady Alessandra a visit, Simeon. Though she's not as young as she was, I'm sure you could shake her up a bit. How Julia might believe the old lady may help her, though, one could only guess. She has no influence these days."

"Julia knows nothing of her grandparents," Isabella stated. "It is something I have never disclosed to her. There is no pride in knowing my father would have used me as a bargaining tool to seek favour with the King. She has no idea she is related to Lady Alessandra. I always told her we had no family left."

Isabella's cold regard for her parents seemed quite understandable to General Martinez; after all, no contact had been made in all the years they had been here working for him. Maybe Lord and Lady Alessandra did not know of their daughter's existence and were under the impression she had perished at the same time as Jacob.

Then, as another idea sprang to mind, and with a hint of a smile, the General said, "Then, the only other connection I can think of is Roscar, where we found you."

Martinez noticed a brief flicker in Isabella's eyes; it was only for a split second, but it was enough.

"Ah! So there it is. Simeon, make for Roscar and the hamlet of Kriel. That's where she's headed. I'm sure of it. That is, of course, if she makes it as far as Roscar. Slim chance for a young girl on her own."

General Martinez left it hanging there in the air – a question for fate or the gods to decide.

Tears filled Isabella's eyes. Simeon sneered at her. Such a pity she was so transparent; he would have enjoyed giving a little physical retribution to the high and mighty Isabella. But for now he must make haste. Too much time had been lost already, though how far could a young girl on her own get? Not too many miles, he decided.

❖

What General Martinez and Simeon had no idea of was that Isabella and her mother had indeed been in contact throughout the years. Firstly, through Mikel and then, to Isabella's amazement, through a hawkwing messenger who had appeared to her one day in the garden, hidden up in the branches of a pear tree. Not long after Julia's birth, she was sat under the tree nursing her newborn baby, deep in thought and grief about what had happened to them – Jacob's brutal and untimely death, the birthmark passed down to Julia as the next in line to the Hamunite throne. What did the future hold for her and her daughter?

In her head Isabella heard a voice, as if in answer to her question.

"Who do you trust?"

"Well, my mother will be worried for me, and also Mikel. She sent him to watch over me, though I have not seen or heard from him since he took Jacob and me to the ship to Hamunite, almost a year ago now."

"Well, give me a message for one or both of them and I will deliver it at once."

I must be going mad, Isabella thought. *I'm actually having a conversation with an invisible friend.*

"I am not invisible, Isabella. Look up. I must stay here amongst the leaves, hidden from those who would bring harm to the land of Hamunite, should an opportunity fall to them."

Isabella looked up and there above her head was perched a beautiful, young hawkwing messenger.

"Oh! I thought for a moment I was losing my mind," she said, as a tear rolled down her cheek. She attempted a smile at the messenger. "I have heard tell of you and your people. Jacob told me all about the hawkwing settlement. He said it was the most beautiful place on all of Hamunite."

Isabella dropped her head to the ground. "Unfortunately, I wasn't allowed to stay long enough to see it for myself," she said, her voice tinged with sadness.

"I can speak to you telepathically and you can answer me in the same way. No one need know of our contact. I am duty bound to do what is best for Hamunite and the people. I know your little one is the next heir to Hamunite, and I am to be your messenger to help others who can protect her well-being. It is in all our interests that only the true heir reaches the island, without enemies accompanying her. Our settlement depends upon this as much as the people of the island."

Taking in all the messenger had said, Isabella decided to speak to her by thought alone; she could never be certain that she wasn't being watched.

"What do I call you?" she asked.

"I am Tia," answered the messenger.

"Well, Tia, it is so good to know you are here. I have felt so helpless. I am a prisoner here. I have no contact with anyone other than General Martinez and his lieutenant, a brute of a man named Simeon. If you can tell my mother and Mikel what has happened to me, they may be able to help me."

"I will take your messages, but know that whilst you are here – whilst you are a prisoner – you are safe from harm. Your child will not have any power until the old king is dying and so they will want to keep her unharmed. For when the time comes, they will seek to use her to gain entry to Hamunite."

"Thank you, Tia, thank you so much. Just one more thing. Can you tell me if the King, Jacob's father, knows about his granddaughter?" asked Isabella.

"No, he does not. Should he find out about her, he might send men to find her and, in the process, put her in danger," warned Tia. "He has already sent a band of men to search out Guardsmen and kill and maim them in response to Jacob's death. However, should you wish it, I will take your message to him, too."

"No, you are right, Tia. Julia must be kept safe at all costs, no matter what it takes. Your counsel is much appreciated."

"I must go now and make haste with your messages. I will be in your head again soon!"

With that, Tia departed, leaving a tinkling laugh in Isabella's head.

Now, almost sixteen years later, Tia was making that same flight to Lady Alessandra, for she had been the same messenger the dairy farmer had called upon to take his vital news.

10

Messengers

As dawn was breaking, Tia circled over the manor house on the edge of the town of Triorey; the home of Lady Alessandra. She floated down to the balcony of the bedroom, where her senses told her Lady Alessandra would be. She tapped on the window and then telepathically called to Lady Alessandra to wake.

Lady Alessandra opened her eyes, knowing immediately who was calling to her, and quickly climbed out of bed to let Tia in. As old friends, they greeted each other, Lady Alessandra taking Tia's small hand in hers. They began their conversation and Tia explained what the farmer had told her and how it seemed that Simeon was searching for Julia.

"What of Isabella?" asked Lady Alessandra.

"I cannot get close enough to the house to communicate with her. There are Guardsmen everywhere, but I know Isabella is inside. I can feel it. I can only assume she is under constant guard," answered Tia.

Lady Alessandra put her hand to her mouth, tears welling in her eyes with worry over her daughter and granddaughter.

"What of Mikel? He has not been in touch with me. Do you know where he is?" she enquired.

"No, but I will search him out. My senses are giving me a strong feeling which will guide me to him," answered Tia. "I will call upon my mate and others from the hawkwing settlement on Hamunite. Together, we will find Julia. She is the being that links us all. She must be found and brought to Hamunite in order to fulfil her destiny. I will need but a short rest, then I will return to my messages and, most importantly, the search for Julia."

"Of *course*," said Lady Alessandra, making for the doorway. "I will get you some food and something to drink. Wait here – I will bring something back to my room. Although I live here alone now and there is only Mary, who comes in each day to help me out, I know the Guardsmen keep watch on my movements and so we must be careful at all times."

Whilst Lady Alessandra was gone Tia closed her eyes and sent out thought waves to Fin, her mate, and other hawkwings who might pick up her thoughts. A smile appeared on her lips as a voice came through to her. It was Fin. Their bond with each other was as if they were one and it never failed to make her feel special.

"I'm with you in mind, but I miss you being by my side. I have realised the seriousness of our quest and am on my way to you now, Tia," he answered.

Tia pointed out to Fin that being seen flying together over the manor house at Triorey could arouse suspicion and so they arranged to meet in a small wood near the edge of the Tovey Mountains. He then let her know the hawkwing community were meeting on Hamunite at this very minute to decide on a strategy in the search for Julia. The strength of her thought waves had reached many and the severity of the situation was not lost on them. The others would make contact as soon as a plan was put together.

11

Danger on the Road

They had travelled for almost two hours before they stopped to rest and eat. In Julia's bag was the remainder of the bread and cheese they had bought from the old lady at the farmhouse, along with the drinking pouch she had filled from the freshwater stream on leaving the farm.

Mikel, as always, was on his guard. He surveyed the area around them, then, climbing over a small stile into a field, he beckoned to Julia to follow him, which she did. After, Julia sank down onto the grass, grateful to rest her legs but most of all to eat something; she was absolutely famished and chewed ravenously on the meagre portions of bread and cheese.

"We'll need to stock up on food before we can begin the climb over the mountains," said Mikel, with a thoughtful expression on his face. "If the weather stays good to us and we don't come across any problems, we should make it to the town of Tovey and the river crossing in two days."

"Is there anywhere to stock up on food between here and the mountains?" asked Julia.

"Yes. At the foot of the mountain there's a smallholding. The family picked the spot especially to sell their produce to travellers who cross over to Tovey. A clever move, though not without dangers," answered Mikel.

"What sort of dangers?" Julia frowned.

"'What sort of dangers?' How naive are you? Wild creatures and thieves! Undesirables of all sorts pass through this way."

Mikel sighed with annoyance. Then, looking into Julia's trusting face, his mood relented and he explained to her the troubles they might face.

"As Simeon searches for you, so too will others, thinking you are of value. There are bad people out here in the big wide world, Julia, and you are going to have to wise up, young lady. On top of that, the mountains themselves pose problems. We will be sleeping out for at least one, maybe two, nights. Wild creatures live up on the mountain and unsavoury characters hide out up there. They might attack us simply to get food."

"I understand, Mikel, and I am grateful for all you are doing for me. I will listen and do as you say, I promise," answered Julia.

"See that you do, but I don't need your gratitude, girl. My love for your mother and her family is what spurs me on. And as it is your duty to get to Hamunite, it is mine to get you there safely."

The intensity of the dwarf's feelings could not be misinterpreted, and so by way of answer Julia nodded back at him. The lump in her throat gave way and she began to sob. The feelings that she had managed to keep at bay rose to the surface like a torrent. This little man's love and pure goodness, despite his usual sharp or mocking manner, had unmasked itself and brought with it the reality of the danger they faced, as well as the weight of responsibility that lay upon her shoulders. Mikel got up and went to her, patting her back in a gesture of comfort and handing her a somewhat grubby handkerchief. He told her to rest for a short time whilst he had a quick scout around to get his bearings.

As Julia lay curled up beside the hedge, Mikel took off to the other side of the field, where there was a small clump of trees. Being small had its disadvantages, but being circus trained had greater ones still. With great agility, he swung himself up into the tallest of the trees, climbing right to the top so that he could see out for quite some distance in all directions. To the west, he could just about make out the tiny dots that were the smallholdings. He estimated these to be some miles away, probably two or three hours at a good walking pace. It would make sense to get to the smallholdings but not venture onto the mountain until the next day. One or two nights up there would be more than enough; no need to risk being in that environment longer than needed. As he surveyed the road ahead and the surrounding area, he could see houses and other buildings dotted around the countryside.

Looking back in the opposite direction, not too far away, Mikel spotted a lone rider on a grey horse making their way down the road which bordered the field. He guessed this was the boy from the barn having caught up with them, which was not surprising since he was travelling by four legs instead of two. If what the boy had said was true, he would expect him to be taking the same route as them to reach Roscar and so he was not unduly worried by his arrival.

However, just as he was about to climb down, something else caught Mikel's attention. Much further back than the boy, he could make out some dots; seven to be exact and then just behind them, a slightly larger one. At the rate they were moving, they had to be horses travelling at a gallop – and the largest of the figures could only be … Simeon! Fast as lightning, he swung down through the branches, hit the ground and ran as fast as his small legs could carry him.

As Leonal trotted along the road, he could see the dwarf running across the field as if the devil was after him. He was just wondering where the girl was when he heard her shout out to the dwarf from the other side of the hedge. He heard the dwarf shout back; the fear in his voice could not go unrecognised.

"They're coming, Julia! Simeon – I'm sure it's him. Riders in the distance gaining on us fast!" he gasped.

Leonal didn't know why – it was an impulsive decision – but he knew he must help them. He turned the horse and, at a gallop, jumped the hedge.

"Quickly!" he shouted to the girl. "Climb on! I'll get you across the field and we can hide amongst the small group of trees. You, little man, you can fit under the hedge. Be quick, they'll be gaining on us whilst you hesitate."

Mikel was in a dilemma. Furious with the boy for taking charge but knowing they had no alternative, he called to Julia.

"Do as he says!"

Turning to Leonal, he growled, "Go on then and hurry! I'll be holding you responsible for her, so take care, boy!" he warned.

Leonal leaned forwards and, gripping Julia's arm, helped her to swing up behind him. They galloped away to the trees on the other side of the field. Mikel, doing as Leonal had suggested, squeezed himself under the hedgerow, hopefully, well out of sight.

Mikel could hear the thunder of the horses' hooves as the riders passed by. After waiting several minutes, he was just about to crawl out from his hiding place when more horses came; from the sounds they made, it seemed as though they were pulling a cart. After a few minutes more, he looked across to the far side of the field, where he could see Julia and the boy emerging, leading the grey mare out from beneath the trees. He signalled them to wait. He needed to get high up in the trees again where, from such a vantage point, he might be able to make out who the horsemen were.

As Mikel made his way across the field, he could see the youngsters deep in conversation – and this worried him. Such a trusting girl, what might she be telling him? On reaching them, he saw the anger on the boy's face.

"You were right to be fearful," Leonal said. "I don't know who you're running from but those men were Bondsmen. Probably stolen the cart and whatever it's carrying. Bondsmen will slit your throat as soon as they look at you."

"Oh, you're an expert, are you?" mocked Mikel, as he swung himself once more up into the tree tops.

"More than you could know!" Leonal growled back at him.

In truth, Mikel knew that Leonal had the right of it – they were Bondsmen. The distinctive way they dressed marked them as such: black scarves tied around their heads and necks; leather straps across their tunics, to which bows and arrows were bound. Were they Guardsmen, they would be easily identified by their red and grey uniforms. The fact they were Bondsmen and not Guardsmen did not make him feel any easier. If they were also travelling to Roscar, the mountains could be even more dangerous than he thought. For now, though, they must move on and make their way to the smallholding at the foot of the mountains.

It had been some time since he had passed this way – in fact, some fifteen years or so, back when he was travelling to Roscar to meet with Tresgar, and many years before that with the circus – but he hoped the family would remember him. If they were still there that was.

Mikel swung down from the tree and as he landed deftly, he was met by Julia smiling at him.

"Mikel, this is Leonal. He is heading to Roscar and has agreed to travel with us," she announced.

"Oh, he has, has he? Well, that's very kind of you, young man, but we don't want to hold you up now, do we? I mean, you've got a lovely horse there that will make your journey much quicker," said Mikel, rather sarcastically.

"It's no bother. No bother at all," replied Leonal, smiling at Julia.

Looking at the two youngsters smiling and staring at each other with soppy grins on their faces, Mikel thought this was all he needed. He knew, though, that there wasn't much point in trying to change their minds. He could tell they wouldn't take any notice of him and anyway, the boy might come in useful, especially as he had a horse. *Well, I could do with a ride and save my legs,* he thought, chuckling to himself.

"We'd better get a move on if we're to make the smallholding before dark," stated Mikel.

So it was that two became three for the journey to Roscar – or four, if you count the beautiful grey mare.

Mikel secured his place riding the grey mare, and Julia and Leonal happily strolled beside him, chatting away. Mikel tried to stay on the alert, but he was also trying his best to listen in to his young companions' conversation. He needed to make sure that Julia did not divulge too much to Leonal. As honest as the boy seemed, they could not be sure where his loyalty lay. The pair had exchanged facts about themselves, finding common ground in their upbringing. Both it seemed had lost their fathers, though Leonal's loss was more recent. This brought out Julia's compassion as she sympathised with him having to leave his mother to go and work in Roscar. She explained that her own reasons for travelling were very similar and she empathised with him as she worried about her mother, just as he did his.

Mikel smiled to himself, for Julia was learning. Though she had not lied to Leonal, she was being careful not to give anything away. Mikel's sense of cool pride quickly evaporated, however, upon the boy's next question.

"Please don't be offended," urged Leonal, "but are you Hamunite?"

Julia was suddenly on her guard. "Why should you ask such a question?" she asked, with a frown.

"Well, look at the colour of your beautiful hair, not to mention those eyes; no full-blood Jahimian has such colouring. I'm guessing you are of mixed blood, though even then, not many of your kind live in safety in Jahimia. You know Hamunites are hunted and imprisoned here, don't you?" he answered, with yet another question.

"Yes, I am aware of this. If by mixed blood and 'my kind', you mean one of my parents was Hamunite and the other Jahimian, then, yes. Does this matter to you?" she asked, feeling rather offended.

Mikel decided that the conversation was getting out of hand and the time was right to intervene.

"Now, look here, young man, what's your problem? One minute you want to help and the next you're interrogating the poor girl."

"No, no, you don't understand," interjected Leonal, holding the horse's reins and halting Mikel in his tracks. "I don't have a problem, but I think Julia may have."

He looked from Mikel to Julia and then back again.

"Please, you have nothing to fear from me. Just let me explain. As I made my way through the forest at the beginning of my journey, I was surrounded by Guardsmen. The leader was a particularly nasty piece of work; he had a large scar running down the side of his face."

Leonal couldn't help but notice the look that passed between Julia and Mikel.

"He wanted to know where I was going and he asked me if I had seen a girl with Hamunite features. Judging by your behaviour back there in the field when you saw the horsemen, I am pretty certain that the girl they are looking for is you, Julia!"

Mikel sighed. There seemed no point in denying it, but at the same time they needed to be careful how much information they shared.

"You have the right of things, young man. The Guardsmen you speak of are looking for Julia. It is of utmost importance that she reaches Roscar but even then, the danger will not be over, for they will pursue her there and beyond."

"What have you done to be hunted down by Guardsmen in this way?" Leonal asked, looking Julia straight in the eye.

Mikel gave her no time to answer. "Done? She has done nothing, other than to be the daughter of a Hamunite."

"Please believe us, Leonal, it is the truth. My only crime is to have a mother who fell deeply in love with a Hamunite who she then married. Shortly after their marriage they were tracked down to their new home in Roscar, where they were preparing for my birth. General Martinez, along with a band of Guardsmen led by his henchman Simeon, killed my father and imprisoned my mother. After my birth, my mother became a servant in the General's household. Well, not even a servant really, more like a slave. She was a prisoner. All of these events have only recently been disclosed to me and my mother has sent me to Roscar with only our very dear family friend Mikel here because she fears for my future and what the General may have planned for me."

Now it was Julia who looked Leonal straight in the eye. "The man with the scar is Simeon. You were right to be wary of him; he has a sadistic streak to his nature. He is not the kind to show mercy. Not to anyone!" she explained.

"I do believe you," Leonal said, "but I also think there is more to your story than you're telling me. I understand you being careful of how much you tell me; after all, we've only just met. I will travel to Roscar with you, Julia, and along with your loyal friend here, I will help to keep you safe. I promise you, you have nothing to fear from me."

"Thank you. Thank you, Leonal. Now we must keep on our way, for if Simeon and his men are following me, I'm sure they will soon be on our trail."

Indeed, Simeon and the Guardsmen were on the companions' trail. Having left Jahim Town at first light, they had already made their way through the forest and were surveying the land from the very same vantage point that Julia and Mikel had the previous evening.

12

The Hunters and the Hunted

Simeon looked down and across the fields to the farm buildings. He surmised that if she had come this way, then it was likely she would have called at the farm for food or indeed to rest. He gestured to his men and they galloped straight on through the fields, thinking nothing of the damage they were doing to the farmer's crops.

The farmer, having just finished his meal, was making his way out of the farmyard when he saw them. Damn Guardsmen, he thought. No consideration for anyone but themselves. How much damage had they done he wondered, their horses' hooves trampling down on his crops. He made his way back into the yard; he wasn't going to leave his wife on her own to deal with them.

They clattered their way into the yard, calling out to the farmer, who was waiting for them, leaned against the door frame of the farmhouse. His wife, also having heard the commotion, opened the door. She was surprised to see her husband standing there and warily assessed their latest visitors.

"What can we do for you, sir?" The farmer directed his question to Simeon, who was obviously the leader.

"We require water for our horses and some refreshments for ourselves while I see if you can help us with some information."

Simeon swung down from his horse and pushed past the farmer and his wife into their home followed by his men.

The farmer and his wife exchanged apprehensive glances and then turned and followed the Guardsmen inside.

"You, farmer, see to the horses and the old woman can get food and drink for my men and I."

Simeon scowled at the farmer. Seeing the look of loathing on the old man's face, he stared straight back and in a cold, threatening manner asked, "As a good and loyal Jahimian, you wouldn't begrudge some basic refreshments to the King's Guardsmen, would you?"

No answer passed the farmer's lips but he went outside to see to the horses with a great feeling of foreboding sitting heavily on his chest. His wife followed suit by getting the food and drink as requested, taking care not to look any of the Guardsmen, particularly Simeon, in the eye.

Some half an hour or so later, having eaten and drank their fill, Simeon sent the men outside to collect their horses. He did not want them to grow suspicious by listening to his questioning. The elderly couple sat side by side on the opposite side of the kitchen table wondering what was to come next. They didn't have long to wait.

"Now then, what can you tell me of any recent travellers coming through these parts?" asked Simeon, his intimidating, large frame leaning over them.

"What is it you want to know exactly?" the old man answered, unable to mask the hostility in his voice.

Simeon leaned in even further. He was not bothered by the fact that the old man had taken a dislike to him. He sneered and, without taking his eyes off him, grabbed the old lady by her hair, forcing her head down onto the table.

"I want to know, old man, of any travellers who may have passed this way in, let's say, the last forty-eight hours or so. In particular, I am interested in a young girl who is missing from home. She would be easy to remember – a cross-breed Hamunite. Not many of them around these parts, I'm sure."

The farmer had not actually set eyes on Julia and Mikel himself, so he could answer truthfully.

"No, sir, I have not seen anyone of that description and that's the honest truth," answered the farmer in a shaky voice.

"I'm inclined to believe you, old man, but it does occur to me she could be in disguise. So, has anyone else passed this way? Now, think carefully before you speak. I don't want to find out you lied and have to come back and deal with you now, do I?" Simeon smiled with pleasure at the fear on their faces as he said this.

They told him of a girl and a dwarf travelling to meet up with the circus and a young man on his way to Roscar to take up work with a family friend. At first, Simeon considered whether Julia could have dressed as a boy until he asked the old man to describe him. A tall, dark Jahimian on a grey horse – it sounded very much like the one they had come across in the woods. As for the circus folk, a girl and a dwarf, he couldn't be sure about them. Anything was possible, although the woman had explained it was dark and the girl wore a hood, which covered her hair, so she had no idea of the girl's heritage. Simeon rode out of the farmyard accompanied by his men, leaving the couple cowering in his wake.

With Simeon now hot on Julia's trail, others searching for her would also be getting closer to learning of her whereabouts.

Fin had reached the small crop of trees at the foot of the Tovey Mountains and was looking out for his love, Tia. He heard her before he saw her; meeting up with her made him smile. He responded by telepathy, "I'm here, waiting for you!"

Before he could say anything more, she soared up in front of him and then swooped down to him, where they enfolded each other, Fin cloaking Tia with his wings.

"I worry about you flying out around this land by yourself," Fin told Tia, holding her close.

"And I worry for you, too," she replied, "but we're together now and there is much we must do. What word is there from Hamunite?"

"Hawkwings have been scouring Jahimia in search for Julia," began Fin. "I myself spotted a band of Guardsmen making their way through the forest below Jahim Town earlier today. I think they could be searching for Julia. Our good friend Kai tells me that he has made contact telepathically with Isabella. She is watched night and day, but the General has decided to put her back to work whilst he awaits news. Apparently, she had been locked in her room under guard. Also, she has had to face some harsh physical treatment. Kai says her face is badly bruised and when the General found out that Julia had gone, in a temper, he threw her to the ground, where she fell unconscious! She told Kai she had sent Mikel to find Julia but she is very worried, as you would expect."

"That explains why we couldn't contact Isabella earlier – if she was unconscious, she wouldn't have been able to hear us. I have been channelling my thought patterns to try to get through to Mikel. I feel he is near, but there has been no answer from him as yet," explained Tia. "I hope he has found her. Goodness knows what might happen to her out here on her own!"

"Shall we put our minds to it and try together?" Fin suggested.

Tia agreed and so the beautiful hawkwing pair settled high up in the trees and closed their eyes, sending out thought waves to Mikel.

13

Old Friends

Julia, Leonal and Mikel were making good progress. They had ventured along the country road, passing by a few cottages, the odd farm worker and some cows lazily grazing in the pasture. As they came over the hill, they could see the sun was beginning its descent into the west. Mikel concluded that it was late into the afternoon. The rumbling of his stomach was also a good clue since it was a while since they had eaten. They were only a mile or so away now. As they made their way down the road, they could see the buildings of the smallholdings and the copse of trees at the foot of the mountains in the distance.

"What?" asked Mikel, seemingly to thin air.

Julia and Leonal turned to look at him. "Sorry, did you want to say something?" she asked.

"Mikel! It's me, Tia!" conveyed the hawkwing.

"Tia, that's wonderful! It's about time some help came along! Thank goodness you found us. I definitely could do with your eyes in the skies," said Mikel.

"You said 'us'. Does that mean Julia is with you?"

"Yes, she is," sighed the dwarf. The thought of having someone to share decisions about Julia's well-being took some of the weight off his shoulders.

"Are you having a conversation with yourself?" laughed Julia.

"No, he's not. He's talking to me!" Tia answered for Mikel.

Julia stopped dead in the road. "Who is that? What are you doing in my head?"

"My name is Tia and I am a hawkwing messenger. Do you know of us, Julia?"

Julia was astonished. She knew of the hawkwings but it was rather surprising to actually have one contact her telepathically.

"Well, yes, Mamma told me about hawkwings when I saw one circling around high in the sky above the garden of the house where we live, or at least where I used to live," Julia said sadly. The fact that she could never go back and the worry of how Isabella was faring rested heavily.

"What are you on about? Who are you talking to?" Leonal queried. "First, Mikel, now you! What's going on?"

"Who's the young man?" Tia asked.

Both Julia and Mikel answered together but this time Julia out loud; Mikel, still wary of Leonal, answered by thought alone.

"His name is Leonal and he is travelling with us to Roscar, where he is to meet up with a family friend."

Although the boy had been helpful, Mikel and Julia were still cautious about telling him the full story of who Julia was.

"What is going on?" Leonal shouted, his hands held out wide in a gesture of helplessness.

"Wait there a moment and you will see!"

Tia's tinkling laughter came loud and clear into Leonal's head.

"Who are you? What sorcery is this?!" said Leonal, in disbelief.

"Oh, get over it, boy! You'll see for yourself in no time."

Mikel gave a short pause. "Now!"

And with that, Tia and Fin appeared, hovering in front of the small group of travellers. Julia and Leonal were awestruck by the sight of such beautiful creatures, but Mikel grinned at them, pleased to have some comrades to share plans with.

"You love to make an entrance, you pair. At least you've shut these two up for a minute or two."

Then, telepathically, he said, "He seems okay, but she's smitten and the way he looks at her, I'd say it's mutual. We must be careful how much we reveal to whoever we meet, however helpful they may appear to be."

Tia looked Leonal straight in the eye. She waited a moment, then spoke to Mikel's mind.

"Your cautious nature serves you well, old friend, but my instincts tell me he is someone who can play a part in getting our future queen home to Hamunite."

Tia turned to Fin. "Do you agree, Fin?"

"I do, Tia. Something tells me this young man has an integral role to play in all our futures."

"Okay," said Mikel. "You've convinced me. If you two think he's okay, that's good enough for me."

And with that, Mikel leaned forward on the horse and slapped Leonal on the back.

"Meet Tia and Fin," he said. "Two of the finest hawkwings you'll ever meet. They are here to help Julia safely on her travels."

Leonal and Julia stared at them in astonishment.

"We're far too conspicuous a gathering here on the road," said Fin. "I guess you're making for the smallholding, so meet us in the small copse of trees at the base of the mountains. There, we can make plans together to get Julia safely to Roscar."

This agreed, Fin and Tia fled and the others carried on along the road to meet them there.

Spurred on by the arrival of the hawkwings, the little group made good time and were soon at their destination. Though tired and very hungry, it was imperative that they stayed on their toes – Simeon could catch up with them at any time.

"First things, first," said Mikel. "We need food and rest. We'll go to the smallholding to eat and stock up on provisions to see us over the mountains and into Roscar. If all looks well, we can stay the night in one of their rooms and set out at first light."

"Okay," replied Tia. "But if anything at all doesn't look or feel right, get out of there! Fin and I will take turns to watch the approach road from the skies. All of you keep your mind open to messages."

"What about you two?" said Julia. "Don't you need to eat, too?"

"Yes, we do, Julia, but we eat the fruit and leaves from the trees. We can forage for whatever we need," Tia explained. "Your kind concern shows me you are everything we need you to be. Thank you. Now, off you go and keep your wits about you."

As dusk approached, Mikel, Julia and Leonal made the short walk out of the trees to the smallholding, which consisted of a good few acres of land, a large Jahimian stone house and, in the adjacent field, large willow-framed round pods, with walls made from straw and clay, which served as places for weary travellers to rest. At the gate of the small walled garden, they were greeted by the delicious smell of cooking. After tying Leonal's horse to a post near to the gate, they knocked on the door and entered into a very large but also busy kitchen. An extremely long wooden table with benches either side was filled with the very men who had sped past their hiding place in the field – Bondsmen!

The men looked up, as they entered the room. One in particular, a physically strong, rugged-looking character with fair to greying hair, took longer to look them over than the others. He held Julia's gaze until she looked away. He registered Leonal's anger and the dwarf's caution before turning back to his supper, apparently unconcerned by their presence.

Leonal had trouble disguising his loathing of the inhabitants of the kitchen. Understanding this, Julia grabbed his hand, which brought him to his senses and deterred confrontation.

A pretty, young woman of about twenty years of age came forward to greet them and offered them a space at the end of the table.

"My mother will be with you in a minute. Can I get you something to drink whilst you wait?" she asked.

"Yes, thank you. We'll take two tankards of ale – and whatever fruit drink you're serving, for the girl," replied Mikel.

As he was speaking, the owners of the smallholding, Daniel and Lucia De Silva, entered the kitchen from the far corner of the room. De Silva was an apt name for Lucia, a woman in her mid-forties; she was beginning to become slightly on the plump side, but her handsome face and black, glossy hair with a streak of silver, swept back from her forehead, made her striking. Lucia noticed the newcomers straight away. A smile came readily to her lips, as she made her way across the room to them.

"Mikel? Mikel Cavellero? Is that you?"

And then, answering her own question, she said, "It is! I'd know you anywhere! A little older, of course, just like the rest of us but yes, it's definitely you all the same." And with that she hugged him with great gusto.

"Put me down, you mad woman!" he said, although the tone of his voice and the genuine warmth in his eyes suggested he was not really annoyed by the show of affection.

"Daniel!" she called to her husband. "Look, it's little Mikel from the circus!"

Daniel made his way over to the little group. He pumped Mikel's hand in greeting and cast a welcoming smile in Julia and Leonal's direction. Not as striking as his wife but, a large powerfully built man, he certainly had a presence about him.

"It's good to see you, Mikel. Why, how long has it been since you passed this way?" he asked, with a thoughtful look on his face. Then, just like his wife, he answered his own question. "Why, it must be fifteen years or more – and you don't look a day older. Well, maybe a little! What brings you way out here? Could it be you are visiting our mutual friend in Roscar? Or maybe you're off to join your folks in the circus? They passed through here only some weeks ago, you know, little friend."

Mikel was not amused by being referred to as 'little' but he let it pass and after he had introduced Julia and Leonal as family friends (without actually calling them by name), they were brought food and drink. Lucia waffled on, reminiscing about past times. This did not bother Mikel too much as it took the emphasis off Julia's presence. He asked what news they had of the circus, in particular his parents. It had been some eighteen months since the circus had been to Jahim Town to perform and it was only natural he missed and worried about them. Although they no longer performed, they were an essential part of the circus, carrying out many tasks and training the new younger artists. They would both shortly be in their sixtieth year and life on the road was tough.

The Bondsmen, having finished their meal and drinks, prepared to leave. Leonal watched their every move, albeit through hooded eyes. Laying down money on the table, the one who had taken the most interest in their arrival went over to Daniel, shook his hand and patted him on the back in a gesture of thanks. He then went to Lucia, and kissed her on both cheeks, thanking her for her wonderful cooking and hospitality. Turning to take in Mikel, Julia and Leonal, he bade them goodnight and wished them an enjoyable meal and a safe journey. Once again, he lingered a little longer on Julia. Then he was gone, with Daniel following.

"You know who those men are?" enquired Mikel.

"Yes, of course. I know what you're thinking – but believe me, Mikel, their reputation is undeserved. Yes, they're fighting men but only when they are threatened," Lucia answered.

"You know nothing!" Leonal raged. "They kill and maim!"

Before he could say any more, Mikel jumped onto the table and slapped him across the face.

"Hold your tongue! You're a guest in this house," Mikel breathed heavily at him.

Leonal's anger did not subside but he did bring it under control. He spelled out to Mikel exactly what he thought.

"Never ever raise your hand to me again, Mikel. And understand this: as the son of an officer of the Jahimian army who was set upon and left for dead, who lay paralysed for the best part of five years until he finally succumbed to his death from his injuries, do not try to tell me that this lady's view of an undeserved reputation is just!"

Julia, stunned by these latest revelations, finally gathered her senses and tried to bring some calm to the situation. She told them both to control their tempers and apologised to Lucia for their behaviour.

Lucia, in turn, said there was no need for apologies; she could quite understand the boy's reaction. She did her best to console Leonal by offering her sympathies over the loss of his father. She could not, however, conceal the troubled look upon her face.

Soon after this they retired to a room set aside for them in the house itself. Leonal lay down on one of the small wooden beds; he kept his back turned to the others, still in obvious fury at the treatment handed out to him by Mikel and at his inability to confront the men who had robbed him of his father.

Mikel and Julia said nothing. They communicated by facial expressions, furrowed eyebrows and shrugging of the shoulders, unsure what to do. Whether they were worried for the same reasons was to be discussed at a later time. Mikel messaged Tia and Fin, explaining all that had happened including the boy's revelation about his father.

Tia told him not to worry about the boy too much and assured him the approaches to the smallholding were clear – the Bondsmen had made their way onto the mountains. She persuaded him that they should all get some sleep for, as promised, she and Fin would remain vigilant, as their eyes in the sky.

And so, while the hawkwings took turns to circle the skies above, Julia, Mikel and Leonal settled down to rest for the night.

Having outstayed their welcome at their previous lodgings, by frightening the elderly farmer and his wife, Simeon and his men followed the same road taken by Julia, Mikel and then Leonal some hours earlier.

Simeon had decided to leave no stone unturned in his search and had ordered his men to search all homes and buildings in the surrounding area. As they were spaced far and wide in and around all the fields and woodland, they had slowed down considerably. Now, in the small hours of the night, tired and hungry, the men had finally convinced Simeon it was time to eat and rest up for a few hours. The closest place for them to do so was almost in sight. As soon as they made it over the rise of the small hill, they would come upon the smallholding.

Fin soared high up in the sky. He was just about to circle back to change over with Tia when he saw them – riders! There were seven of them, their outlines clearly visible by the light of the moon. He stretched his wings wide, pulled them back and launched himself into flight, making his way back to the copse of trees where Tia was waiting, messaging to her and Mikel as he flew.

Tia, whose telepathy had been known to span much further than the average hawkwing, received Fin's message immediately, but Mikel had fallen into a deep sleep due to the ale he had consumed earlier in the evening. Tia decided to try Julia instead. She was woken instantly by the voice in her head. Quickly, she jumped out of bed. They had all slept fully clothed in readiness for a quick getaway. She roused the other two as quietly as she could for they did not want to alert anyone in the household to their departure. Leonal was soon ready and Mikel, though rather jaded, managed to lead them as noiselessly as possible out through the back of the house. Here, he and Julia scurried across to the trees on the other side of the road while Leonal collected his horse, which Daniel had stabled for him after seeing the Bondsmen off the premises. Tia and Fin urged them to make for the mountain, even though it would be difficult terrain to travel over during the night.

As they began their ascent, Simeon was banging on the door of the house at the smallholding, rousing everyone from their beds.

Daniel, opening the door in his nightclothes, was not unduly surprised to find Guardsmen at his door. Patrols often came this way in search of Hamunites trying to make their way into Roscar – and with the Bondsmen in the area, it was possible they were tracking them.

"We're looking for a place to eat and rest, and maybe you can help us with some information," Simeon said.

"Of course, sir," replied Daniel. "Please come in. If you settle yourselves here at the table, I'll bring ale and then get my wife to come down and find you good men some decent fare to eat."

Daniel was playing the perfect host, but still there was no fear in his voice or body language. He knew he was able to look after himself well enough if required. While Simeon and the Guardsmen sat drinking their ale, he went to get Lucia and fill her in on their latest visitors.

"Be careful of what you divulge. They're after something, or someone, and I think I have an idea who it might be. As I passed by Mikel and his friends' room, I noticed the door was ajar. I looked in – they're gone, all of them."

Lucia busied herself by feeding the hungry Guardsmen with the ever-full pot of soup made from seasonal vegetables. She cut them large hunks of homebaked bread and cheese, also made from their own produce at the smallholding. The men were ravenous and soon set about clearing their plates. Daniel addressed Simeon.

"Sir, I have a spare pod with enough beds for you and your men. If you would care to follow me, I am sure you will have a comfortable night's rest. I have taken the liberty of stabling your horses and providing them with feed and water."

"Yes, that will be fine," Simeon replied. "Lead the way."

Once at the pod, the men seemed happy enough with their accommodation, but as Daniel made his way back across the field, Simeon called out to him to wait a moment. He whispered to one of the Guardsmen to wait until he had returned inside the house with Daniel and then for them to search all the remaining pods in the field. As Simeon caught up, he put his arm around Daniel's shoulder. With Daniel being a rather tall man, the impact of Simeon trying to unnerve his host with this gesture was lost. Daniel was on his guard, but his manner betrayed nothing.

"What can I do for you, sir?" he asked.

"Just a little of your time, my good man. I am in need of information about people who may have travelled this way recently. Let's go inside, shall we – where we can talk in private," answered Simeon.

Fortunately, Lucia had already returned to bed and their daughter Helene had remained in her room. Simeon seated himself at the long table while Daniel filled two tankards with ale. He passed a tankard to Simeon and then sat down.

"So, sir, it's very late and tomorrow I have a busy day, so can we get down to what it is that you want to know?"

Simeon smiled across at him; the smile, however, did not reach his eyes. This was not lost on Daniel.

"I am looking for a girl who has run away from the home of General Martinez. I believe she may be either travelling with a dwarf or in disguise as a boy."

"Well, you understand we have people passing through here all the time but, yes, I do recall a dwarf. Something to do with the circus, I believe. Whether or not he had a girl with him, I couldn't say, and as for a girl disguised as a boy, well, if the disguise was a good one, how could I tell?"

Simeon had the distinct feeling that the man was playing a game of sorts but his head was fuzzy, probably from the ale. He suddenly felt extremely tired. He tried to look Daniel straight in the eye except it was difficult to stay focused, so he thanked him for his hospitality then took himself back to the pod, where he lay down and fell asleep in seconds. The sleeping draught Daniel had secretly added to Simeon's ale had done its job. Daniel sighed; he hoped Mikel and his young friends were safely on their way.

With Tia and Fin on high, keeping watch over the smallholding and scanning the surrounding area, Julia and the others picked their way along the mountain path by the light of the moon. Although the days were unusually warm for spring, the nights were considerably cooler, and small patches of snow and ice had formed further up the mountain. Leonal bent down and offered his hand to assist Julia over a particularly tricky patch of icy rock.

"Why do the Guardsmen want you so badly?" he asked.

"I cannot tell you, at least not at this time. If you knew the whole story, it could put you in danger," she replied.

Once they had negotiated the difficult patch of ground, he let go of her hand.

"Oh, and I suppose travelling with you isn't putting me in any danger then?" Leonal said, with a certain amount of sarcasm. He was still feeling aggrieved at Mikel.

"Of course it is, but the more you know, the more they could get out of you –and believe me, it's not just about saving my own skin. There are many whose very existence depends upon my reaching my destination safely," she answered.

Leonal nodded, resigned to the fact she would not open up to him, at least not just now. His instinct told him to be patient. He could not put a name to the feeling he had about her but he knew, somehow, he had to keep her safe. As dawn began to break, they could see the smallholding below them. They knew it wouldn't be long before Simeon and his Guardsmen would be tracking them once more.

14

Allies

Progress up the mountain was slow in parts. Julia walked beside the horse, as Mikel rode with Leonal, guiding it carefully through the rocks, shrubs and bushes that decorated the mountainside. To continue on their route through the mountains and on into the river town of Tovey, they would need to go through a mountain pass with high rock faces on either side. This was dangerous as they could be easily ambushed. Knowing that Simeon and his men were still some way behind them eased their worry, but only slightly, for this place had a reputation for being roamed by bandits – particularly Bondsmen.

The sun had begun to rise and the mountain ice was melting. The three travellers started to make their way through the mountain pass. Tia and Fin had remained behind to keep watch on Simeon and his men. They had also sent out messages to other hawkwings, although the further they ventured from Hamunite, the more difficult this became.

Kai, a fellow hawkwing, knew this, so had flown down across the forest, to the trees overlooking the farm. Here, he was able to pick up the thought waves of his fellow hawkwings and communicate with them. He bade them a safe journey, promising to return once he had delivered the news of Julia to her mother, grandmother and the rest of the hawkwing community back on Hamunite, as well as those who had flown further afield in the search for Julia.

Simeon was awakened by a mixture of laughter and shouting. As he tried to sit up, he groaned, holding his aching head in his hands. Surely he hadn't drunk that much ale? He could hear his men outside and made his way out of the pod to see what was causing such noise. One of his Guardsmen was dangling a child of about five or six by his ankles. The child was thrashing about, trying to hit him. The rest of the Guardsmen found this a source of amusement.

"What's going on out here?! Can't a man rest without this disturbance?" Simeon growled.

"Sorry, sir, but the boy here was sneaking around our pod. I thought I'd teach him not to be so nosey," answered one of the Guardsmen.

During this exchange the boy's mother, with other offspring in tow, made her way from her own pod over to the commotion and began remonstrating with them over their ill-treatment of her child.

Simeon's head was banging and this made his temper even fouler than normal. "Keep your brat under control! If my Guardsmen had mistaken him for something else, he might be minus his head by now!" he snarled at the woman.

He turned to the Guardsman and gave the order to release the child, which he promptly did by dropping him on his head. The mother rushed to her child and quickly ferried him away, along with his siblings, back inside their pod.

"Did you search the pods?" Simeon asked.

"Yes, sir," answered the Guardsman who had tormented the child. "No Hamunites of any description to be found."

Simeon ordered his men to make ready the horses and collect supplies; they had spent enough time here and they needed to make haste. If the girl had help, she could already be over the river and into Roscar.

He went up to the house and upon finding a trough of cold water in the back yard, submerged his head in it. As he shook off the water, he was met by Daniel coming out of the back door.

"Landlord, I thank you for your hospitality. Here is payment for our food and lodgings," he said, handing Daniel a small bag of Jahimian coins. "Though your other guests would do well to keep their brats under control … anyway, what we discussed last night about the dwarf and the girl – have you or your family recalled anything else?"

"No, sir. My wife and daughter, like myself, remember a circus dwarf and a few young men on their way to and from Roscar passing through but that is as much help as we can be, I'm afraid," Daniel calmly answered.

Simeon nodded. He would not pursue his questioning of this man any longer. Enough time had been wasted and he knew the man was not of the sort to be intimidated easily, so he and his men set off up the mountain trail.

Observing their departure from the tree tops, Fin and Tia took off, high up into the sky, but they were immediately spotted by one of the Guardsmen.

"Look!" he shouted. "Hawkwings! A pair of them! I've never seen them so far into Jahimia before."

The significance of the hawkwings was lost on the other Guardsmen as they had no idea who they were hunting. For Simeon, however, this was a breakthrough. He now knew he must definitely be on the right trail. He was certain wherever the hawkwings were, Julia wouldn't be far away.

Tia and Fin, knowing they had been spotted, made haste to catch up with the others.

Up on the mountain, other interested parties had also been observing the progress of the travelling trio. The Bondsmen, having left some hours before them, had secreted themselves high up on the rocky face of the mountain pass, where they lay in wait for their prey.

Julia, Mikel and Leonal were almost halfway through the pass when the hawkwings caught up and told them that Simeon and his men were hot on their heels. Tia sent out messages asking for help from any friends from Hamunite who might be in the area. Her call was answered by what would seem an unlikely source.

As Simeon and his men reached the opening of the pass, he gave the order to pick up pace. It wasn't long before the galloping of hooves could be heard in the distance. Fin, high above, could see the rapid progress the Guardsmen were making and urged Tia to hurry Julia, Mikel and Leonal onwards as their pursuers were mere moments away.

Suddenly, from the opposite direction, came the echoing,

high-speed sound of horses. The small group of travellers stopped still. Tia hurried to Fin to see the situation for herself.

"What's happening?" Mikel called to them.

"Keep going, my friends. Help is at hand," Tia told Julia, Mikel and Leonal, who was still struggling to get used to someone being in his head.

He looked up, as the help Tia had spoken of made its entrance around the corner of the rocky pass. It was the Bondsmen! Was she mad? Five of them charged straight past while the one who seemed to be the leader and who had spoken to them the previous evening stopped and spoke directly to Leonal.

"Hurry, boy! Get them safely through the pass. On the other side there are some caves set back in the rock. Hide them there. God willing, we will be back to guide you on into Roscar."

With that, he was gone, charging after the rest of his men, leaving Leonal open-mouthed at the audacity of a Bondsman giving him orders. Tia flew down, urging them to do as the Bondsman had said. They could hear the clash of swords and the whinnying of horses, as they were forced into battle. Leonal did as he was asked and they were soon out of the pass, where he could make out the caves the man had spoken of some short distance away.

Back in the pass, Simeon and his men were met with arrows raining down from above. The experienced soldiers that they were, they merely raised their shields and kept on going. Only one of his men, riding at the rear of the party, received an arrow, to his thigh. On turning the next corner of the pass, they were met by the rest of the Bondsmen. Immediately, the fight began. Swords clashed and horses hammered their hooves, as their masters controlled them as they fought. Shouts of anguish, as men were wounded and knocked to the ground, mixed with screams of dying horses. Both sides fought with determination and great dexterity – these were well-trained fighting men.

Simeon had only one thought in mind: to get through the pass. He made progress through the melee and, coming alongside a Guardsman, motioned to him his intent to escape the fight and seek their prey, and for him to cover his exit. Born to take orders, the Guardsman nodded in agreement. With some swift strokes of his sword, he cut his way through and made it out onto the other side. The leader of the Bondsmen, seeing Simeon's intent, attempted to go after him but was cut off by the Guardsman, who pressed him back into battle. The Bondsman had no choice; he must defeat this nuisance of a Guardsman in order to pursue Simeon.

Tia and Fin had been surveying the scene from above. Fin stayed behind to see how the Bondsmen fared while Tia trailed Simeon.

Simeon cantered off through the pass and, looking over his shoulder, he could see that his orders had been followed. He smiled to himself. She would soon be his. He knew now she could not be much further ahead. Oh, how he was looking forward to showing that little madam who was boss.

15

The Beast

They found the series of caves the Bondsman had spoken of, at the beginning of the downward journey towards the valley that lay between the Tovey Mountains. They jumped down into a ditch which ran parallel to the mountain track, and there they were, openings of all shapes and sizes. The largest was at the very end of the ditch, which then led out onto a shelf and a sheer drop down the side of the mountain.

"What do you think?" Leonal asked Mikel and Julia.

"I think we should set the horse loose and make our way as far into the cave as possible on foot," Mikel replied.

"Why lose the horse?" asked Julia. "The cave looks deep enough to take her with us."

"No," said Leonal. "As much as I hate to say it, Mikel is right. If the horse gets spooked, the slightest noise will give us away. I'll send her off down the track. She won't go far and with a bit of luck, we'll be able to pick her up again on our way down."

Leonal led the horse a short way down the track, where he slapped her rump hard in an effort to get her to run off, to which she duly obliged. Meanwhile, Julia and Mikel began to make their way deeper into the cave. At each twist and turn, they came upon more and more astounding sights: deep caverns with high roofs that glistened with encrusted crystals, and a sparkling stream flowing gently through a gully. Mikel tasted the water and declared it as fresh as could be. They both bent to drink in this much appreciated moment of respite.

Leonal was making his way back to the cave when he saw Simeon come galloping out of the pass. It was clear that his adversary had seen him in the same instant. Realising he could not make for the cave in time, Leonal decided to stand his ground and drew his father's sword. On reaching him, Simeon pulled his horse to a halt and unsheathed his own sword.

"Do you really think you stand a chance against me, you fool?" he mocked. "You should have gone to the keep and offered yourself up for training, as I suggested. I never forget a face, boy. You're with her, aren't you? A damned Hamunite. Your father will be turning in his grave."

"You know nothing of my father!" Leonal countered. "He would have been appalled to see a bully such as you hunting down a young girl. And for what? What can she have done that is so bad to warrant Guardsmen chasing her across the whole of Jahimia?"

"She hasn't told you then…" Simeon smirked. "Well, far be it from me to be the one to enlighten you. Shall we get this over with?"

Simeon lifted his sword and charged. Leonal was swift-footed and agile; he sidestepped the strike and ran up the rock face, somersaulting over his opponent. While moving through the air, he lashed out with his sword and caught Simeon on his upper arm before landing behind him. With a grimace, Simeon made a backwards stabbing motion. Leonal felt the blade slice across his cheek. Blood dripped down his face. Simeon, realising the tight confines made battle from horseback impractical, dismounted and lunged towards him, where they began to trade blows in earnest.

Back at the cave, Julia and Mikel were beginning to wonder as to what was taking Leonal so long. Mikel tried to get Julia to stay while he went to investigate but she was having none of it. As they crept their way closer to the mouth of the cave, they began to hear the clash of steel.

"Oh my goodness," whispered Julia. "It could be Guardsmen, or Bondsmen, or both! I hope Leonal isn't caught up in it."

She ran towards the opening. Mikel tried to grab her, but she was too quick for him and so he followed her instead. The sight that greeted them made Julia call out. The swordsmen turned to face her.

"Stop!" she shouted. "Leave him, Simeon! This is not his fight."

"Ha! He should have thought about that before he drew his sword. Furthermore, I understand that this fool doesn't even know he's escorting the future Queen of Hamunite!" Simeon announced in great delight, taking in the look of incredulity on Leonal's face.

They had each dropped their swords to their sides, as the exchange of words took place. Leonal turned to face Julia.

"You're to be Queen of Hamunite? I don't understand. I know you are of dual blood and the hawkwings..."

He stopped, his face a picture of enlightenment.

"Of course! The hawkwings! I should have realised you were more than just an ordinary girl!"

"Yes, yes, very interesting I'm sure, but now, Julia, you know you must come back with me. This game of yours is over. The General himself will escort you to Hamunite," declared Simeon.

"Over my dead body!" came the voice of Mikel, as he stepped out of the cave entrance.

"Well, if it isn't the milkman. Over your dead body, you say? Well, that can be easily arranged, little man!" snorted Simeon.

Tia was surveying overhead. She focussed on getting messages to Fin and the Bondsmen regarding everything she had witnessed.

Simeon began to advance upon them, when suddenly, out of the cave, came a roar. All four turned to see, stepping out into the sunshine, the most extraordinary of creatures: a dog-like beast, twice the height and width of a man. Its humongous head shook, and its massive mouth barked. Frozen, they all stared at the creature. The beast pounced forwards and in a split second had tilted its head to one side and scooped Julia in its mammoth jaws. It launched itself off the mountain shelf and down into the drop below.

16

Pursuit

"Julia!" The anguish of Leonal's cry echoed throughout the mountainside.

Tia was first to react, swooping down to tail the creature. Leonal and Simeon both tentatively moved to the edge of the cliff shelf and peered over; Mikel sat stunned, his head in his hands. The astonishing sight that greeted the pair at the edge was something neither of them could have possibly imagined. The creature was walking vertically down the mountain! Julia looked up at them, waving her arms. Simeon ran to his horse, quickly mounted and headed after them, making his way back along the ditch and up onto the mountain track.

Three of the Bondsmen came out of the pass. The leader was bloodied from the fight and had Fin flying alongside him. They were already aware of what was happening as Tia had communicated the goings-on to Fin throughout. The Guardsmen had been defeated. The only two to survive were retreating along the mountain pass. Two of the other Bondsmen, though battered and bruised from the battle, had gone after them. The archers who had lain hidden on top of the pass had stayed behind to keep watch for other unwelcome parties. Leonal was shaking Mikel, shouting at him to get up.

"Look! Look over the cliff face! We need to get down there as quickly as possible. It's walking down the mountain! Julia is still in its mouth and she's alive!"

"It's the Grippon!" the Bondsman leader called to them. "I don't know why it should take her, but certainly not to eat her – it's a herbivore. Where's your horse, boy? We must hurry!"

After quickly explaining about his horse, it was decided they would double up; Mikel joining the leader on his horse and Leonal riding with a young man, maybe a year or two older than himself. The third Bondsman put all of the travellers' belongings onto his horse and joined the pursuit.

They followed the mountain path and tried to keep Tia in their sights, chasing not only the Grippon and Julia, but also Simeon, who by now had a decent head start on them. Although he too was following Tia, knowing that she would lead him to Julia, he would not have the advantage of her messages. These would be for Fin and only those that had the good of Hamunite in mind.

The Grippon's paws concealed its huge suction pads underneath. Julia, head and feet dangling either side of the Grippon's jaws, was petrified. Apart from the fact she was encased in its mouth, the descent was terrifying. She could see Tia gliding backwards and forwards across the downwards path the Grippon was taking. Tia tried to message the Grippon, but its concentration on the task it was performing blocked her out. Tia's presence was of some comfort to Julia, although how the hawkwing alone could release her from the jaws of this great creature, she could not imagine.

"Julia, be brave. Fin tells me Leonal, Mikel and the Bondsmen are on their way. I will stay with you and guide them to you," Tia told her.

This message gave Julia hope. She knew Mikel's loyalty was without question, and instinct told her the same could be said for Leonal – but what of the Bondsmen? What could be their reason for coming to her aid? Tia responded to her thought patterns.

"The Bondsmen are Hamunites, Julia. They came to Jahimia on the orders of the King, when your father was killed. This is not the time for explanations. I ask you to trust me, Julia. The Bondsmen will give their lives to protect you."

The Grippon carried on down the sheer face until it reached a sloping incline, which gradually became less and less acute, until eventually, it was walking horizontally. Julia had fallen faint. The creature picked up speed. Tia had done well to keep up, for neither she nor Fin had rested much the previous night. However, as the Grippon went further into the forest, she lost them. She circled the area before deciding she would have to go down into the forest. Fin pleaded with her to wait until he caught up, but she argued they could not waste time.

"Simeon is closing in fast. I must find them before he does!"

With that, she swooped down. It was moss-laden and damp beneath the trees. The further she went the darker and denser it became. She flitted between the low branches, looking for clues. She could sense and glimpse other creatures hiding. Shaggy-haired, monkey-like beings with the snouts and teeth of boars appeared from the higher branches, snapping at her. She hoped they were just being territorial and would not see her as actual prey. Then she heard the squawk of a mountain eagle. Now, she really was worried. Should the eagle decide she was a threat to its territory, she would be in major trouble.

Simeon had reached the edge of the trees and was cautiously picking out a path, looking for signs that the Grippon had come that way. He knew that the tracks of such a considerable creature would be easy enough to find. He was right: broken branches and flattened grasses pointed to the way the Grippon had taken her. Tia was fortunately a step ahead of him and had discovered the signs further into the forest. Eventually, she saw an opening and came out to a beautiful lake adorned by mountain greenery and heathers. She was just in time to witness the Grippon, on the other side of the lake, release Julia from its jaws. She rolled out of its mouth, covered in slimy drool, onto a patch of long grass. Tia was just about to message Fin, when she noticed large ripples on the lake heading closer and closer to the bank where Julia lay.

"Fin! Hurry!" Tia messaged. "Are the others keeping up with you? I do hope so, for I think we may have more to worry about than just the Grippon and Simeon!"

"Hold on, Tia. We are entering the forest now. I will fly above and be with you in minutes, my love."

Tia flew up to greet her mate but before she met him, two things happened at once. Out of the lake emerged a man of gigantic proportions. Shaking the water from his huge head of hair, he climbed up onto the bank, towering over Julia while the Grippon lay down beside her. Meanwhile, from out of the skies, came the eagle Tia had heard screeching earlier. Startled, she tried to fly out of its reach but she was not quick enough. It fastened its talons to her shoulders and coasted higher into the sky, heading back up onto the mountain.

Fin had witnessed the eagle snatch Tia. His heart thumping in his chest and blood rushing to his head, he went to fly after her, messaging that he was on his way. She was his life: he had to save her. The close bond the pair shared made Tia somehow more fearful for her mate than for herself. Should the eagle, or indeed its mate – for, like hawkwings, they were most often found in pairs – attack him, they would stand little chance of escape. She knew to struggle would be futile and that she must wait until they reached the eagle's nest, where she hoped it would set her down; then, she would be able to turn and face it, and use her hands and feet to defend herself.

Remembering the mission at hand, Tia messaged Mikel and told him what was happening, both in the skies and on the ground. She urged him to take great care and to trust the Bondsmen, as well as Leonal, in their quest to free Julia not only from the Grippon but also, she informed him, the mountain giant that had emerged from the lake.

"Should Fin or I not message you again, my friend, try to make contact with other hawkwings. Our dear friend Kai promised to fly further into Jahimia to keep in contact with us. He will help you in our place," she said sadly. "Julia is the most important being for all who live on Hamunite. You must succeed in this, Mikel. The alternative is too terrible to imagine."

"Oh my! Tia! Fin! There must be something we can do?" Mikel cried.

"Your destiny charts a different path, my friend. If the gods are with us, we shall meet again. If not, well, I believe everything happens for a reason."

And then her voice was gone from Mikel's head.

"I pray for you both. May we be together again soon," Mikel messaged back to the hawkwings. He could not conceal his despair. Neither of the hawkwings answered, so he did not know whether his farewell had reached them. The dwarf's face was a picture of anguish.

"What is it, Mikel?" implored Leonal. "What's wrong?"

Mikel sorrowfully explained to Leonal and the others the plight of their hawkwing friends and the latest developments on Julia. The leader of the Bondsmen quickly took charge. He discharged the man carrying the travellers' supplies to free his horse of all the extra weight and sent him back up the mountain in search of the hawkwings.

"If you need to, use your bow, but only if it is a choice between the lives of the hawkwings and the eagle," he said. "The creature should not be harmed unless it becomes absolutely necessary."

"Understood, Macki," replied the Bondsman and then was on his way.

"So, *you* are the legendary Macki Bond?" Leonal sneered. "I thought it might be you."

"And I know of you too, Leonal, but this is no time for explanations. We must put aside all else until Julia is safely back with us; she must remain our priority at all times," Macki returned, without threat or malice in his voice. "Now, onward! We need to get to the lake – and quickly!" he commanded.

Despite his loathing of Macki Bond and his surprise at the

Bondsman knowing who he was, Leonal knew he was right; he must remain in control of his feelings for Julia's sake.

Simeon, who was a short way ahead of Julia's allies, came across the same creatures that had snapped at Tia. Only, this time, the creatures must have thought the human a bigger threat, for they attacked him wholeheartedly, jumping on his back and biting at his neck. Using dual swords, as he rode through the trees, steering his horse by knees alone, Simeon quickly dispatched the ugly boar-headed monkeys. He ran his sword through two of the creatures then flung them away into the trees; the other animals, alarmed by the ferocity of the assault, shrieked and squawked, scarpering back up into the trees, leaving Simeon to ride on.

As the others made their way further into the forest, they too were attacked. Macki, leading the group of travellers, adopted a different approach. As the creatures leapt onto them, Macki ordered Mikel and Leonal to take fruit stored in the saddle bags and throw it to the floor behind them. This proved to be enough of a distraction. Macki explained that the tree pigs, as he called them, were only trying to chase them out of their territory. Being particularly greedy vegans, they wouldn't be able to resist the food. They didn't, and the creatures soon left them to carry on their way.

Try as he might, Leonal couldn't help but be impressed by Macki's knowledge. First, the Grippon; now, the tree pigs; and what about the order he had given the Bondsman to help the hawkwings. None of this added up. It certainly wasn't in keeping with the Bondsman's reputation.

On reaching the clearing which led down to the lake, they could see Simeon already on the other side, but there was no sign at all of Julia, the Grippon or the giant.

"We will split into two parties to go around the lake. Mikel, you come with me to the right. Aaron—" Macki called to the young Bondsman, "you take Leonal to the left with you and we'll meet on the other side. Draw your swords and stay on guard."

On spotting them, Simeon decided to get away from the area, though he was puzzled as to where the Grippon had taken Julia. He needed to formulate a new plan; nothing could be achieved by him staying here to fight with the Bondsmen. He could see them coming, but this side of the lake was towered by another mountain. He needed to move quickly before they penned him in, so, mounting his horse, he set off in the direction of Aaron and Leonal. He surmised that the weight of the two men on one horse would slow them down more than the one carrying the dwarf and his rider. He was hoping to get far enough around the lake to head back into the forest and track the way he had come. The two young men saw Simeon just ahead of them, as he turned into the forest.

"Should we go after him?" Aaron asked Leonal.

"No. As much as I would like to, finding and rescuing Julia is more important than anything or anyone else at this moment in time," he answered.

They pressed on, looking for clues and keeping their swords drawn. When they finally reached the other side of the lake, they discovered Mikel and Macki were already there. Mikel sat astride the horse, as Macki searched around for signs.

"We saw Simeon! He headed back into the forest," Leonal said, as he swung down from Aaron's horse. Macki nodded in acknowledgement but took up searching the area, concentrating on the job at hand.

"Have you found anything?" Leonal asked.

"Well, this is the spot where Tia messaged Mikel – for sure. The long grass has been flattened and there is a very wet trail, which must have been made by the giant Tia spoke of. It seems to go right up to the rock face and then disappear. There must be an opening of sorts somewhere here. They can't have just walked through the rock. Everyone spread out and feel your way around. Look for anything, however tiny, that doesn't look or feel right," Macki ordered.

It seemed as though Julia, the Grippon and the giant had indeed disappeared into the mountain. Macki took his sword and, using the hilt, began to tap on the rock. Leonal immediately understood what he was doing and quickly copied him. Using the hilt as a hammer would identify where it was hollow, which could mean a hidden cave. There it was! The hollow sound they had been searching for! Leonal called to the others.

"Here! There's something here!"

On closer inspection, they could see some markings, where the rock had been scraped. A slightly raised edge, which Macki traced with his fingers in an arched shape, went well over his six-foot frame. They guessed that this must be a way inside, but how to get in was another matter.

17

Behind the Stone

Julia was indeed trapped inside a large cave behind the rock face. The giant, upon reaching the shore of the lake, had seen the Grippon lying in the long grasses with Julia beside it covered in its saliva.

"What have you done, Grippon?" the giant asked, staring down at the small figure of Julia.

"I have saved her!" it replied defensively.

The giant knelt down beside her. He gently wiped the thick saliva from her face with his huge hand and put his ear to her mouth.

"I can't hear or feel her breath," he said anxiously.

With a dexterity belying his size, he opened her mouth wide and with a single finger, pressed carefully upon her chest. Nothing happened, but then he tried again and this time he saw it rise. She made a small coughing, gurgling sound. He lifted her up into his arms, as though she were no more than a feather, and made his way to the face of the mountain; the Grippon following.

Julia slowly opened her eyes to see that the gigantic dog had been replaced by a gigantic man. She lay in his arms, quietly staring up at him, unable to comprehend what had happened or indeed what was happening now. He placed her down and seeing her awake, spoke to her in a deep yet gentle voice.

"Do not be afraid. We mean you no harm. My friend the Grippon thinks he has saved you, though from what I have no idea."

Julia just stared up at him, trying to make some sense of it all.

The giant leaned into the rock face, causing it to grind, and then, as if from nowhere, a large entrance was revealed. The opening was an arc shape, which fitted perfectly and pivoted from the centre. He picked her up and took her inside, resting her down on a fur rug. He lifted a torch from the wall and, using a piece of flint, made a spark to light it. The Grippon placed its rump against the rock and closed the entrance.

The large cave now lit, Julia could take in her new surroundings. There were piles of furs in one corner, and weighty pots and a jug next to where she lay. A table, taller than herself, with a woven basket filled with fruit, sat in the centre of the cave. Next to the table was a giant-sized wooden chair on which the giant now sat, with the Grippon on the floor beside him.

"What do you want with me?" Julia asked.

"I saved you," the Grippon answered in its slow, deep tone. "The ugly one, he wanted to take you. He say you be Queen of Hamunite. The young one, he fight to save you. I help."

"Oh, right. Well, I see. So, you don't actually want to eat me then?" she queried.

The Grippon opened its eyes wide, shocked she could ever think such a thing, while the giant shook his head, chuckling to himself.

"Young lady, my friend the Grippon here is no killer. In fact, he eats nothing but vegetation from the mountain trees. I hope that puts your mind at rest. Believe me, you are in no danger from either of us."

The giant handed Julia a bowl of water which, in his hand, seemed tiny, but in hers was huge. Using both hands, she tilted it towards her mouth and drank deeply. She had not realised how thirsty she was.

"I do however have a question for you. Is my friend being fanciful or did he misunderstand what was happening to you? For I cannot understand where he would get such a story as to say you are Queen of the sacred island of Hamunite."

"It is complicated. Grippon, you were right about the ugly one. His name is Simeon and he wants to capture me to take me back to Jahim Town, where he will hand me over to General Martinez, who thinks I can help him reach the island of Hamunite," she explained. "So, yes, in a way you did save me, but my friends, the young man you spoke of and others, they are trying to get me to Roscar, where an old friend of my mother and father will hopefully have some answers for me."

"You have only partly answered my question, my dear," the giant stated. "What of the claim that you are to be Queen of Hamunite?"

Julia looked at the giant and the Grippon, as she weighed up how to answer such a question. After a short silence, she decided to be as honest as possible with them, in the hope that they really were no threat to her or her journey.

"My father was killed before I was born. He was the son of King Joalian of Hamunite. He came to Jahimia to make peace between the two countries but fell in love with my mother, a Jahimian. They were banished by my grandfather, hunted down by General Martinez and after murdering my father, he enslaved my mother while waiting for my birth. He thinks the power of the tide of Hamunite will pass to me on the death of my grandfather. These revelations are very recent to me, although I understand my mother has kept many secrets in order to keep me safe. So, yes, if this prophecy should prove to be true, I am the future Queen of Hamunite."

Having spoken this out loud for the first time, it suddenly seemed all the more real to her. The giant and the Grippon exchanged thoughtful glances.

"So, Grippon, it seems you did indeed save the young lady," said the giant.

"Told you I save her. Now we help her. Then maybe she help us," the Grippon answered.

"Okay, introductions first," began the giant. "This is my good friend the Grippon. That is what he is but it is also his name, for he is one of a kind. I am Pascal, the last of the mountain giants of Tovey. We look out for each other, like family, and so you see, Julia, we understand how it feels to be alone, to be hunted because you're different."

Julia was feeling much recovered, and relieved that she was not in immediate danger, but she worried about her friends and said as much to Pascal and the Grippon. The Grippon admitted it hadn't really had a plan but had just acted on the spur of the moment, not really considering Julia's companions.

"I must find them," Julia said.

"Then we will come with you to look for your friends," said Pascal. "I also think we should join you by offering our services in helping you reach your destination safely. What say you, Grippon? Do you agree?"

"Of course!" it declared happily. "Hoped you say that. How exciting!"

This decided, they began gathering a few provisions, when suddenly they heard tapping on the cave entrance. They all turned towards the sound and stared at the wall.

"Were you followed, Grippon?" asked Pascal.

Julia answered, telling Pascal that Tia, the hawkwing, had been travelling above them and would have led the others to her. After pausing to think, Pascal ordered the Grippon to shield Julia while he pushed open the entrance to his home.

"Be prepared to act, Grippon, just in case those who would harm our new young friend have tracked you here, too. Are you ready?"

The Grippon, looking suitably sheepish, replied, "Ready."

Pascal leaned against the rock and pushed open the entrance.

As the cave began to reveal itself, the four men stood poised, swords at the ready. Pascal came out, towering above them, and signalled for them to hold back.

"State your business!" the giant demanded.

"Our business is the well-being of our friend – the young woman you and the beast you were seen with have taken. She had better be okay or you will be sorry!" shouted Leonal.

Julia suddenly appeared from behind Pascal and ran into Leonal's arms, the Grippon close behind.

"I'm fine, honestly I am. The creature you speak of is called the Grippon and he thought he was helping to save me from Simeon."

Julia smiled up into Leonal's face. Turning to face the rest of the companions, she gestured to Pascal.

"This is Pascal, the last of the Tovey giants. Pascal and the Grippon know who I am and why I am here. They want to help."

The men all lowered their swords and sighed with relief. Their bodies relaxed, now that they knew they would not be fighting giants and beasts. Macki took in each and every one of this strange-looking band. Maybe this extra help would prove useful, but he would need to observe their characters for some time to decide who could be trusted to do what to help safely transport this precious young woman. Mikel went over to Julia and took her hand. She hugged him tightly in return. After telling her how relieved he was to see her safe, he then gave her the distressing news about Tia and Fin.

"What can we do? We must help them!" Julia agonised.

Macki came forward and led Julia to a nearby rock and sat her down. Kneeling in front of her, he took her hand in his.

"Your Highness, I am a Hamunite, sent to Jahimia some years back to act as a protector of sorts for other Hamunites who left their homeland to make a new life in Roscar. I have lived in and around these mountains for many years now and know them as well as any man can. My friend and compatriot Donald knows exactly where to find the eagle's nest. He is a master archer, as are all of the Bondsmen. We spend our days in constant practice of the skills we need to survive the lifestyle we have chosen. He will find the hawkwings."

"But will he find them in time?" Julia whispered.

"We must not give up hope," he replied. Standing up, he turned to face Julia's newest friends. "Now, giant, you say you wish to help. We are out of supplies, so some food and water would be most welcome, if you have some to spare?"

"Of course. We catch fish from the lake and we also have plenty of fruit. As the Princess said, the name is Pascal. I have lived in these mountains all my life and I already know who you are, Macki Bond," he replied.

The two of them smiled a smile of mutual respect. While the giant went to get the food, Macki gave Aaron orders to build a fire; he told Mikel to try messaging the hawkwings; and he asked the Grippon to climb the mountain and keep a lookout for friend or foe.

"And what would you have me do?" Leonal asked.

"You and I need to talk, my boy," Macki replied. "Come walk with me." His tone suggested that this was more of an order than an invite.

Leonal's chest was tight and his head ached from trying to keep his anger under control. Surprisingly, he wasn't angry with Macki for maiming his father, but rather with himself. He was struggling with his conflicting loathing and respect for this man.

"I know you blame me and my men for the injuries your father sustained during that skirmish some five years ago," said Macki. "I also know your father, a man for whom I have the deepest respect, died recently and so I understand that being in my presence at this time must be particularly difficult for you. However, you do not yet know the full story of Captain Jules Mathius."

Leonal turned and faced him eye to eye and hissed. "How dare you even speak his name!"

Macki remained calm. "I dare because, unbeknown to you,

Jules Mathius was my friend and this story was supposed to be told to you by Tresgar on your reaching Roscar. Unfortunately, things have developed at a much faster rate than any of us could possibly have envisaged. So it is, Leonal, that I ask you to hold your tongue – and your temper – for a little longer while I try to explain."

Macki held Leonal's puzzled gaze for a second and then turned to walk around the lake. Shortly after, Leonal began to follow him.

Macki began. "I was part of Prince Jacob of Hamunite's guard. The prince, who you now know to be Julia's father, was a great man. He wasn't just our leader but also a dear friend. We grew up together and trained together in combat skills; skills all young Hamunite men must learn in order to defend our sacred island. After the fragile new treaty between Hamunite and Jahimia fell through, Julia's grandfather, the King, in his anger, banished Jacob and Isabella from the island. They made their way to Roscar, where they were given work and befriended by none other than your father's friend Tresgar."

Leonal's expression registered surprise at this but he said nothing; his interest and curiosity aroused, he was eager to hear more. Macki went on.

"Shortly after he banished them, King Joalian, having calmed down and thought things through, realised the danger he had put his son and heir and his wife-to-be in. He sent me, along with a small band of Hamunite defenders, to go after them and bring them back. By the time we found them, it was too late. General Martinez had led a group of Guardsmen into the Republic of Roscar, murdered Jacob and abducted Isabella, Julia's mother. We found out all that had happened from Tresgar, who had discovered Jacob's body and Isabella's disappearance the next day. A former Guardsman himself, he saw the signs of their work and made discreet enquiries. His main worry was for Isabella, for he knew that she was carrying Julia. We decided that any rescue attempt would only put Isabella and her unborn child in danger. My men and I remained here in Jahimia to help other Hamunites who might need safe passage into Roscar and also to be on hand for when the time came for Julia to take up her birthright. The hawkwings decided that King Joalian should not be told of Julia's existence because, since word of his son's death, his mind had become unbalanced and his decisions unpredictable. His orders were for me and my men to carry out revenge attacks on Guardsmen. We knew that this would only put Julia in danger and so we decided to stay and help other Hamunites travelling through, while remaining ever-ready to come to her aid when needed.

"The hawkwings will only message with those who have the best interests of Hamunite and its inhabitants at heart. It was when you arrived at the smallholding that Tia made me aware of what had happened. Tresgar moved freely between Roscar and Jahimia, seeking help from your father. They decided that General Martinez had gone too far, but to confront him or King Jared, whose vanity in losing Isabella to Jacob had cancelled out any rational or moral thought, would have been suicide. Instead, along with my men and others, who wished for peace between the two countries, a secret allegiance of like-minded beings was formed. Those involved worked hard to keep safe the Hamunites who came here to make new lives. The Guardsmen were and still are under orders to detain any Hamunites they may find for questioning. What that actually means is torture, to find ways to gain entry to Hamunite – something no one can tell as the only way to gain entry is for the true ruler to turn the tide."

Leonal hung on Macki's every word.

"One autumn morning, some five years ago, at the foot of the Tovey Mountains, by the smallholding you recently passed through, your father was on his way back from a visit to Tresgar, when he saw a small band of Guardsmen attack two travellers. They were pulled to the ground and tied to the back of their horses to be dragged along the track. Your father, being the kind of man he was, intervened. The leader of the party of Guardsmen became angry at your father's interference and the two drew swords. The fight was in progress when I and a few of my men approached from the other direction. The rest of the Guardsmen had formed a circle around them but, on seeing us approaching, quickly mounted their horses and charged at us. The fighting that day was fierce and though we sustained injuries, none of my men were killed. The only surviving Guardsman was the leader who had been fighting your father. He charged off, leaving your father lying on the ground. I set off after him and an arrow drawn from my bow brought him down. Your father had fallen from his horse and landed awkwardly on a rock at the side of the road. It was a freak accident that paralysed him.

"Our friends at the smallholding, Daniel and Lucia, did all they could to help. We waited for nightfall and then Daniel and I took your father home in Daniel's cart. The three of us decided that – in order to keep safe you, your mother and others involved in the allegiance – we would say your father was attacked by my men. So, it has become that the stories of Bondsmen attacking Guardsmen have grown over the years when, in fact, there have been so many times when we are supposed to have been involved in skirmishes in which we have not even been present."

Macki's story finally came to an end. Having listened intently, Leonal asked, "Why didn't he tell me?"

"As I said, he wanted to keep you and your mother safe. It was better that you believed the stories, too. That way, you could not be compromised," answered Macki.

"But I would never have told! I can't believe he didn't trust me!" Leonal agonised.

"Now, that's your youthful pride talking, boy. You know your father did what he did for only the very best of reasons and that his trusting of you was never an issue. He and Tresgar made a pact that when he died you would pursue your father's work. The fact that Julia's destiny has called at this moment in time makes me believe that your paths are entwined. That you chose freely to join her and Mikel without any knowledge of our plans lends heavily to this. Your actions, from what I have seen and what Mikel has told me, have all been based on instinct. This instinct is serving you well, Leonal. I will leave you to contemplate all I have told you. Any time you wish to talk with me, I will be here for you but, for now, let us join the others. Darkness is falling fast and we need to eat and rest."

Macki turned to make his way back to the rest of their companions, with Leonal following deep in thought.

18

The Eagle's Nest

The eagle's talons plunged like a knife into Tia's shoulders. A trickle of blood ran down her chest and onto her feathered torso. The pain was unbearable.

Fin messaged and messaged.

"I'm here, Tia. I'm right behind you. Everything will be fine. I will attack it from behind as it arrives at the nest. That will distract it long enough for you to get out of there. Okay, Tia? Tia, talk to me!"

But Tia had fallen unconscious.

Feeling her pain added to his distress but it made him all the more determined to save her. Fin sensed the eagle knew that he was there but was not going to let go of his prey to challenge him. In the short time they had been flying back towards the first mountain, the eagle had begun to soar higher and higher. They had flown over the mountain pass and up towards the peak where, some fifty metres or so below, Fin had made out the eagle's nest. Unfortunately, the nest looked occupied by the eagle's mate.

"Tia, you must wake up! Please, my love. I need you to help me!"

Fin knew he would be no match for both eagles by himself and that he and Tia would surely be made a meal of. Not only was the air much thinner this high up the mountain, it was also much colder. An icy blast to the face brought Tia back around, and hearing Fin's voice gave her new strength.

"I'm okay. Please be careful, Fin," she told him.

"We get out of this together, Tia. You know we come as a pair. Now, do as I say. We only have one chance. We must get onto their backs and then hold on for dear life. As he drops you into the nest, I will jump on his back. I think his mate will try to help him. That is when you must get on her back – while she is distracted. We will only have seconds to do this, Tia. They will swoop high and low, to shake us off. Our only chance is, when they get as low as possible, to jump and head for cover on the ground. Can you do that, Tia? Are you strong enough?" he asked.

"Fin, for you I can do anything. I will be ready, my love," she answered.

"Okay, Tia, we're almost there. Get ready," he told her.

The eagle dropped Tia into the nest. In a split second, Fin had landed on the eagle's back and just as he predicted, his mate emerged from the nest in order to help him. Tia knew this was their only hope and so, summoning all her strength and ignoring the pain in her shoulder, she too rose out of the nest, and landed on the female eagle's back. The hawkwings wrapped their arms tightly around the eagles' necks, and dug their knees and feet in, holding on for dear life, as they banked from side to side. The eagles thrashed and the hawkwings clung, on until eventually they all began to tire.

"Be ready, Tia. When I say let go, head for the small clump of trees towards the mountain pass."

"I understand, Fin. I'm ready when you are," she replied.

As the eagles descended, tired by the weight of the hawkwings, Fin shouted, "Now, Tia, now!"

Both hawkwings let go of their hold and glided down towards where Fin had seen cover. The eagles were strong creatures and once they had lost their burdens, they quickly regained their composure and went after them, gaining on them fast. Terrified, Tia and Fin held each other's gaze for a moment and then, with as much effort as they could muster, dived towards the trees. Suddenly, from out of nowhere, arrows rocketed one after another, making a divide between the hawkwings and their pursuers. The eagles shot off, enabling the hawkwings to make it to the safety of the trees.

Once they were beneath the shelter, Fin pulled Tia to him, holding her in a tight embrace until she made a small cry of pain. Releasing her, he could now see the extent of her injury and this worried him terribly. There was a small hole in her shoulder, from which blood was flowing, matting the feathers on her torso. Fin heard a noise behind him. It was Donald, one of the Bondsmen. It was then he realised where the arrows had come from.

Donald knelt beside Tia. He quickly took a clean piece of cloth from his pocket and pushed it into the hole in Tia's shoulder. She winced and cried out in pain.

"I'm sorry, my dear," Donald said, "but we must stop the flow of blood."

Then, he turned to Fin and told him what he thought they should do. "The best thing would be to take her back through the pass to the smallholding, where Lucia and Daniel can care for her."

Fin realised that this was the only real option with Tia being so badly injured. With Donald's help, they made their way back safely through the pass to the smallholding where, as fortune would have it, their good friend Kai was also heading to, in the hope of finding them.

Donald cradled Tia in front of him, as he rode his horse back through the pass. Other Bondsmen signalled to him from their lookout posts so he knew they were clear to pass through. On reaching the smallholding, Fin received a message from Kai to say he was close at hand in the trees opposite the house. Daniel and Lucia willingly took over caring for Tia. Hawkwings were not used to living in houses, so they took her to the bed in the attic – which to her was enormous – from where she could see the mountain in all its glory.

Kai flew in through the open window to see for himself the extent of Tia's injury. After some discussion, it was decided that Donald would join the other Bondsmen up at the mountain pass to keep an eye out for the coming and going of suspicious characters. Kai would take over from the hawkwing pair and join up with Julia and her ever-growing band of protectors. Promising to be careful and to keep out of sight of the eagles, he set off. A strong young hawkwing, he soon made his way over the pass, smiling to himself, as Mikel's voice came through to him.

"Hawkwings of Hamunite, we need you. Your fellow hawkwings Tia and Fin need you. If you can hear me, please make contact."

"Hello, Mikel. I am Kai, a friend of Tia and Fin, and I bring you good news. The hawkwings are safe, though Tia is injured and in the care of Daniel and Lucia De Silva, with Fin by her side. I am on my way to join you and the rest of your party. What news of Julia?"

"Oh, such wonderful news you bring. Julia is safe. The creature that took her was trying to save her from Simeon," answered Mikel. "We are resting by the cliff face on the mountain lake. Night is falling fast, Kai. Be careful of the eagles and other creatures of the mountain woodland that do not take kindly to we intruders."

"Do not worry, Mikel, I am almost with you. I fly low to the trees but not so low the creatures amongst them can reach me, and I think the eagles will be back in their nest after my friends tiring them out. They will need a good night's rest themselves," Kai chuckled.

As he came towards the forest where the tree pigs lived, he saw Simeon ride out, heading back towards the mountain track, picking his way slowly down towards Tovey. He immediately messaged Fin, who was not unduly worried as Simeon was now a man alone. However, he made it clear that Kai should pass this information on to Macki and the others.

As Kai came upon the lake, he could see the glow of a campfire across the water, close to the second of the mountain faces. His senses were heightened by the excitement of the task which he must now undertake for the future of the inhabitants of Hamunite. He must not be found wanting. He flew low to the lake, trailing his fingers in the water, elated at all this freedom; freedom to venture so far from home. He could imagine the older hawkwings' response when Fin got closer to home and messaged everything that had happened. Oh, that youngster with all that responsibility. Fin and Tia had faith in him. Fin would reassure them and, after all, no other hawkwing had flown this far, so it was down to him and him alone, at least for now.

Approaching the shore of the lake, he raced higher into the sky and messaged Mikel that he was arriving so that the other members of their party would not be startled. After passing the message to everyone, Mikel confirmed it was clear to land. He swooped down, landing on a large boulder which Julia was resting her back against. As she turned to face him, he gave a dramatic low bow, using arm and wing.

"Your Highness, I am Kai, at your service."

Julia smiled at her newest guardian.

"Welcome, Kai. I am most grateful for your service, as you put it, but I'm not sure I warrant being called Your Highness. However, your skills will prove to be a great help to us all, I am sure. Now, can you please tell us all what has happened to Tia and Fin. We have all been very worried about them."

The newest, and indeed the youngest, member of this strange group settled down with his newfound friends to tell them the tale of Tia and Fin's escape from the eagles.

19

Circus

Simeon made his way back through the woodland and out onto the mountain track. He knew to try and take the girl by himself was no longer viable, certainly not while on the mountain. He would need to wait for a more opportune moment. He decided to go on ahead of Julia and her protectors. He would lie in wait for them on the other side of the River Tovey. From there, he felt he would have the upper hand and would just have to wait for his moment to take her. He pushed on through the night and by early morning light was crossing the bridge into the town. Taking in his Jahimian Guardsman's dress, the Regimental Keepers of Roscar, who guarded the bridge, asked him his business in Tovey. He assured them he was only looking for a place to rest the night and so they let him pass. Knocking on the door of the nearest inn, rousing a tired and irritable landlord, he finally stopped to rest. But not for too long, he thought to himself – oh no, he must be ready for them when they passed this way.

Over on the mountain, as the sun began to rise, Julia and her companions were beginning to stir. After packing some provisions, they set off, skirting the face of the second mountain and making their way down towards the River Tovey and the town. They were a strange-looking bunch: a young girl, a dwarf, a giant, three men, the mighty Grippon and a hawkwing messenger. This time, the Grippon offered Julia a more comfortable ride, high upon its back. Its warm, soft, shaggy hair was comforting to her as she leaned forward and nestled her face into its neck. The Grippon felt a happiness it could not explain. All it knew was it was glad it had saved her.

During the early morning light, the grey mare had somehow found her way to the lake. Leonal was delighted to see her. Mikel rode the horse while Macki, Leonal, Pascal and Aaron, who the rest of the group had now been informed was in fact Macki's son, made their way on foot, leading the two remaining horses packed with supplies. Kai flew above them; eyes, ears and mind open to all around him.

On they went, keeping a good pace as they climbed down the second mountain, making very few stops to rest and eat. It was mid-afternoon when they finally made their way down to the river crossing. There were two, or perhaps for extremely strong swimmers, three ways to cross. The first was a wooden bridge, which was guarded by the Keepers of Roscar. The second was a towing ferry half a mile or so further down water. Macki explained it would be closer and easier to go straight across the bridge but because the bridge would take them directly into the middle of the town, meaning they could be noticed, he advised they take the second option and head to the ferry.

Kai sailed high enough up into the sky that from below he would look like a bird. Hawkwings were not known for flying so far from Hamunite and this would almost certainly cause a stir. On arriving at the ferry, it was soon apparent that they would not all fit; indeed, the Grippon would need two ferries just for himself. Pascal sorted out the matter, with his ever-calm and sunny disposition.

"The Grippon and I can easily swim across. We are quite used to swimming in the mountain lake. You take care of yourselves and the supplies, and we'll see if we can beat you to the other side," he said laughing.

The ferryman's interest was roused by this strange group of travellers and he knew it wouldn't be long before the Keepers of Roscar would be asking him who had used his ferry that day.

"You lot with the circus?" he asked.

"Yes, that's right," answered Mikel. It was easier to let him think this.

"Thought so," said the man. "They've been on the other side of Tovey for the last few days but, of course, you probably know that."

"Yes, of course, though we are not sure of the precise location as we were delayed slightly, so if you can point us in the right direction, that would be most helpful," Mikel replied.

It would be a real bonus to meet up with the circus, he thought. Not only would he get to see his parents and old friends but it would provide a good cover for this conspicuous bunch of travellers. Simeon had been foiled, but he was sure it wouldn't be long before there was a bounty placed on Julia's head. Then, all sorts of characters would be sure to show an interest in them.

Pascal stripped down to his trousers and passed his clothes to the others to take across for him, and lined up next to the Grippon, slightly up water from the ferry, which was waiting for them to depart.

"You ready, Grippon?" he said to his friend.

"Guess so," it replied in its laid-back drawl.

As the ferry and its passengers pulled away, Pascal turned to the Grippon. "Come on then, let's show them what we're made of," he said.

Show them they did. While the ferryman pulled his ropes, the man-mountain and his huge, hairy friend powered their way through the water with ease, reaching the other side with time to spare. When they were all safely deposited on the other side of the river, Pascal got dressed and the Grippon divested itself of the water logged in its fur, with a shake that nearly soaked the friends. They set off in the direction of the circus, as shown to them by the ferryman.

The circus, it seemed, was camped on the other side of town and so this meant they would have to pass through the centre and the busy marketplace, scuppering their chances of keeping a low profile. As they made their way through the market, they stopped at a few stalls, buying extra provisions to add to the salted fish and fruit in the bags carried by the horses. People stopped what they were doing. They took steps backwards, as they stared up at the Grippon and Pascal. The rest of their group, Julia included, appeared of no interest by comparison, except to one pair of eyes hidden in a doorway.

After making their purchases, the band of travellers went on through the cobbled streets of the town, which then opened up onto the fields and countryside of Roscar. They could see the red and yellow of the colourful big top tent, beautifully lit by natural sunshine in a large field not too far away. Mikel found his excitement mounting at the thought of seeing his family and friends after such a long time; it was truly lifting his spirits.

In no time at all, they had made their way down the country lane and were there in the field at the big top, among brightly coloured caravans. There were open fires on which large pans emitted delicious smells. There was a vibrant atmosphere made up of people of every shape and size. Some were sat chatting while others were practising their arts, such as fire-eating and tumbling, but as Mikel and his friends made their way through the crowds, people began to turn and stare.

"Mikel!" called a voice behind him that made him turn and grin. Then she was there, his mother! Her arms wrapped around him. His father appeared, laughing out loud, absolutely delighted to see their son. Mikel turned to Julia and the others.

"It is my pleasure to introduce my parents, Magdalena and Alfonso," he announced.

He introduced the group as his travelling companions, not giving away any clues as to who each of them was. The curiosity of the circus people was mainly directed at Pascal and the Grippon who, being one of a kind, left even the circus folk fascinated. This meant that Julia, merely a human girl, was of no real interest to anyone – aside from the owner of the pair of eyes that had followed the companions from the market and was still watching her every move.

Finally satisfied at being able to see, touch and hear the Grippon speak, the circus folk went about their business, with the promise of seeing the travellers at the show later that evening. The group were taken to a corner of the field, where Mikel's parents' beautifully decorated caravan stood.

"So, Mikel, what are you doing here and why are you travelling with such an odd group?" asked his mother.

"Well, that's a fine thing to ask when you and Papa travel with a right menagerie of characters and creatures all the time," he answered.

"I know, I know. But seriously, Mikel, I'm thrilled to see you. We both are. You know that. But what is it? Something is going on. I feel trouble is either here with you or fast on your heels."

"Let's leave my friends to eat and rest, then I'll fill you in."

Nodding to Macki and scanning the area around them, Mikel and his parents went into the caravan to talk privately.

When they emerged from the caravan, Magdalena walked over to where Julia was sat talking to Leonal and Aaron. She laid a hand on Julia's shoulder and bent forward to speak quietly into her ear.

"Come, child. Come to the caravan with me. I have something for you."

Julia smiled at the two young men and got up to follow Magdalena. When she reappeared, both boys chortled. They went over to her and playfully slapped her on the back, for Julia was now dressed in a young man's tunic and leggings and her head was covered by a scarf which tied at the back, covering the birthmark on her neck.

"Who is this come to join our merry band I wonder?" mocked Aaron.

"Oh, I'm not sure. What's your name, lad?" Leonal joked.

"Enough, you two. Show some respect," said Macki, coming over to join them. "However, Your Highness, this is a good idea.

Hopefully, this disguise will help you blend in more easily. And keeping your hair covered is a good idea."

"I think I am going to get used to being a boy quicker than I am to people calling me Your Highness," Julia said. "But really, Macki, the boys are only teasing. If you treat me like one of them, I will blend in even more."

"Very well," Macki replied. "It may also be a good idea for me to teach you how to defend yourself. I will show you how to use a bow and arrow, as well as a sword."

"Oh yes, please!" Julia replied excitedly.

"I can teach her," Leonal cut in.

"Yes, I'm sure you can, Leonal. We can all take turns to help Julia," Macki answered, flickering a smile.

Leonal was obviously smitten with Julia but he wasn't sure how this relationship could develop. After all, the girl was to become a queen.

After they were fed and rested, they were invited to watch the show in the big top. Night had descended. The moon and stars glistened in the sky, as they made their way to the evening's entertainment. Julia felt relaxed for the first time since leaving what had been her home. Almost at once, the feeling was replaced by one of guilt, as she thought of her mother. Leonal smiled at her.

"You okay?" he enquired.

She nodded and put the feeling to the back of her mind. The Grippon, too large to join in the audience, had to be satisfied with poking its head through a gap that had been specially made for it in the side of the tent – though the people of Tovey who had come to see the show thought it to be part of the circus and stared at it in amazement.

The show began and the ringmaster introduced the acts one by one. The crowd marvelled at tumblers, bareback horse riders, fire-eaters and trapeze artists, cheering and clapping them all. Then came The Illusionist.

He walked around the ring; a tall man with dark, swarthy skin, thick, black eyebrows and eyes of deepest brown. A large gold hoop hung from his left ear and from his right, what looked to be a large, sharp tiger tooth. His costume was made up of shiny silver and gold fabric, as was the tall turban he wore. He gestured to the ornate, rectangular table and chairs standing in the circus ring. Then he spread his arms wide, as he made a great show of taking in each and every one of the audience. Finally, his eyes rested upon Julia and he smiled.

"Young man, would you care to join me and astound this wonderful audience with a great illusion?" he asked.

The others were immediately on their guard.

"No, I don't think he would," Leonal called. "But I would be happy to help you out. My cousin here is very shy."

Macki nodded his approval of Leonal's handling of the situation. However, neither of them had bargained for Julia's naive and inquisitive nature.

"Don't be so silly, I would love to help," she said, quickly jumping up out of her seat and into the circus ring before any of them could grab her.

Macki groaned and leaned across to whisper to Leonal, Mikel and Pascal.

"Keep your eyes on her at all times," he told them, before turning to his son. "Aaron, you come with me. We must secure the outside of this big top and warn the Grippon to look out for anything that doesn't seem right."

"Father, are you sure you're not overreacting?" Aaron asked, once they were outside the tent.

"Why, out of a full audience, should that magician pick Julia? Answer me that," Macki replied.

"I understand you being jumpy but it is most likely just a coincidence, or maybe, since he knows we are friends of Mikel and his parents, he just wants to make us feel welcome?" Aaron suggested.

"I hope you're right, Aaron, but I have a bad feeling about this and without making a scene, I can't physically remove her from the ring. That would just bring more attention to us. As if we haven't caused enough of a to-do already, arriving here with the Grippon and Pascal," he sighed. "I will inform the Grippon to keep its eyes open, and you and I will keep guard around the outside of the big top. If we go around in opposite directions, we can cover the area and let each other know of anything untoward. Okay, Aaron?" Macki asked.

"Okay, Father," Aaron replied. And they set off in opposite directions around the big top.

Meanwhile, inside, the show was still going. The Illusionist waved his hands in a mesmerising manner and then, picking up the two wooden chairs, he placed them on top of the rectangular table, one at each end. Taking Julia's arm, he turned her to face him.

"Look into my eyes," he said. He then took the tiger tooth from his ear, tapped it gently on the palm of her hand and proceeded to swing it back and forth in front of her eyes until she was hypnotised.

She followed his commands one by one until finally, with his help, she lay her body down, suspended between the two chairs. The audience, including Julia's band of protectors, were silent and the atmosphere was charged with anticipation. Then, slowly, theatrically, he began to unwind his shiny turban. As it unravelled, it coiled into a mass of fabric at his feet. When, finally, his head was bare, he lifted the shimmering fabric from the floor and flung it out in front of him before whirling it like a cape above his head, allowing it to obscure Julia, the chairs and the table. He walked around the table, arms aloft, drawing the audience's eyes to the covered body. At the front of the table, he grabbed at the fabric, then removed it with a sweep of his hands. She had disappeared.

The audience gave a hearty round of applause while Leonal, Mikel, Pascal and the Grippon waited with bated breath for him to replace the fabric and bring her back. Instead, with one swish, he covered himself and in a twisting motion, the fabric fell to the ground and he, too, was gone.

20

The Illusionist

The big top appeared to have become frozen in time as Leonal, Mikel and Pascal, along with the rest of the audience, watched aghast, waiting for some resolution. The spell was soon broken, though, when the Grippon let out a roar and surged forward towards the circus ring. The big top began to creak and sway, as the Grippon ploughed into the arena, tearing out the tent pegs.

"WHERE IS SHE?" it boomed. Screams and shouts abounded, as people scurried to get out of its way. Leonal, Mikel and Pascal were already searching the area; checking under the chairs, table and shiny fabric of the turban.

"There's nothing!" Leonal declared. "She's gone. He's gone. They're gone! Do you hear me? Gone!"

"I know, we can see, too, but you must calm down," Mikel stated. "We need to think straight, and quickly. Time is of the essence. Come on, we need to get out of here and find Macki and Aaron."

Outside, the two Bondsmen rushed around the big top, meeting at the place where the Grippon had poked its head through.

"Something is wrong. Did you see anything? Anything at all?" Macki asked.

"No, nothing. We best find the others and see what's happened," Aaron replied.

Together, they lifted the heavy tent and ducked inside. They were greeted with chaos – and it was easy to see why. The Grippon was pacing, and Pascal was trying to calm it down. Mikel was trying to do the same to Leonal. The rest of the audience were fighting their way out, as the tent began to collapse around them. The members of the circus sprung into action, holding poles upright inside and heaving on the tent ropes outside.

"Has she been taken?" Macki called to Mikel.

"It would seem so. He made her disappear, then disappeared himself. We cannot see how or where they have gone," Mikel explained.

"Leonal, Grippon, pull yourselves together!" Macki ordered. "We need to act quickly. Mikel, gather your parents and any of the circus folk they trust. Search the site, the caravans, tents, everywhere – leave no stone unturned. Leonal, Pascal and Grippon, you search all the surrounding area, though it is likely he has taken her back through the town. Simeon may have put a price on her head. Aaron and I will head back that way."

"I will come with you!" Leonal demanded.

"We don't have time for this!" Macki snapped back. "Aaron and I know this land. We pass through here all the time. Obey my command, boy! I know what I'm doing. We need to move. Mikel," he said turning to the dwarf, "where has Kai been hiding while all this has been going on? Message him, now!"

❖

The young hawkwing had flown many more miles than ever before in his life. He was so weary he had declined to go to the show. Thinking it best he kept a low profile, he had landed high in a tree on the edge of the field, where he had fallen sound asleep. The roar of the Grippon woke him. It took him some seconds to realise where he was as he had been dreaming of home, up in the treetops of Hamunite. Through the darkness, he spied a rider racing towards the town. Something was going on over at the big top, and it looked like it was falling down. It was then when Mikel's voice came to him loud and clear.

"Kai, where are you? Julia has been taken! Answer me, damn it!"

"I'm here, Mikel. You say she's been taken – when? How did this happen?"

"If you had been doing your job, maybe with your incredible eyesight, you would have seen something!"

Mikel was angry and frustrated at having been outwitted. It came to Kai then.

"There was a rider travelling fast towards the town. I'm on it now. I will catch him up easily. I'm sure he must have something to do with it. I can feel it."

"Well," replied Mikel, "do that and start using your telepathy to get in touch with Julia. Macki and Aaron are also heading for the town. They are mounting up as we speak."

Kai launched himself into the air and was soon flying at great speed, with the hooves of Macki and Aaron's horses pounding along the road behind him, but he was so fast that he soon left them behind. He was quickly upon the town and could make out a number of different riders far below, making their way in and around.

"Julia, where are you? Can you hear me?" he called to her. There was no answer but he could feel her presence, as he swooped lower and lower, finally coming to land on the rooftop of a large town house.

Opposite was a row of smaller houses and at the end, an inn. An archway led into a courtyard which housed stables and the entrance to the inn. Kai flew across the lane onto the stable roof. He tried again to contact Julia. Still nothing, yet all of his senses drew him to this place. She was here somewhere. He was sure of it. Macki was coming through to him, asking if he had any news.

"I'm at the inn opposite the large town house near the market. I haven't reached Julia but I'm sure she's here. I can sense her."

"Okay, we're almost with you," Macki replied.

In no time at all Macki and Aaron were trotting through the archway into the courtyard. Dismounting quickly, Aaron went to search the stables while Macki went inside in search of information. Kai remained on the rooftop, watching and listening for any signs of Julia. Aaron came through to his mind.

"She's here! I've found her, but she seems to be in a deep sleep."

Aaron clicked his fingers and gently tapped her face. She began to stir. As she looked at him, the frown on her face showed a state of confusion. Suddenly, Kai messaged back.

"Be careful, Aaron. Two men are making their way to the stables. I shall inform your father."

While Macki was distracted, talking to the landlord, Simeon had been making his way down the stairs with The Illusionist when he spotted the leader of the Bondsmen. Putting his finger to his lips, Simeon gestured to the magician to follow him and they crept out of the building to the stables. As they entered,

Aaron was ready for them, standing between them and Julia, with his sword drawn.

"I don't know how you did it," he said to The Illusionist, "but if you leave now, no one need get hurt."

The Illusionist threw back his head and laughed while Simeon sneered, "You really think you can take on both of us?"

He raised his sword and lunged. Aaron responded, matching him blow for blow, but then The Illusionist took the tiger earring from his ear and, dancing from side to side, he waited for an opening in the sword play. Quick as lightning, he stabbed it into Aaron's neck. Aaron put his hand to his wound and dropped his sword. He stood still in a trance, his sight blurred. Simeon lifted his sword to cut him down, just as Macki arrived to block the blow that would have surely finished Aaron off.

Following Macki into the stables, Kai settled in the rafters and notified Mikel and the others about what was happening. In no time at all they were on their way to help. Macki and Simeon fought on. The Illusionist watched, waiting for an opening, tiger tooth in hand, ready to pounce and drug Macki at first chance.

Julia was by this time starting to come round from her drug-induced sleep. She could not quite understand what had happened or indeed what was happening, but she realised Aaron and Macki were in serious trouble. She also recognised Simeon and this alone was enough to jolt her out of her confusion. Standing up and backing further into the stable, out of the corner of her eye, she saw a large pitch fork lying amongst the hay. The Illusionist, following her eye, lunged forward at the same time as her. As he tried to stab at her with the tiger earring, she stood on the fork, causing the handle to spring up between them, catching him on his shin and making him stumble. As he fell towards her, Julia jumped backwards, sending the forked end catapulting up and piercing his throat. For a moment, everything froze – the look of utter surprise on his face and the horror on hers. Then, his body fell forward. His limbs and torso collapsed to the ground, but his head remained skewered to the pitch fork, elevated above the rest of his body.

There was a brief recess in the fighting. Macki and Simeon looked on at the gruesome sight of The Illusionist, before shifting their stance. Macki placed himself between Julia and Simeon, who looked at her in amazement before quickly recovering his composure. He had no feelings for the magician other than as a means to help him reach his goal, and here that goal was. She was his only reason for being this far south and crossing into the land of Roscar. He needed to get her back to Jahim Town, to General Martinez.

As Julia stood there, stunned by the horrific death, Simeon resumed the fight. Macki fought back vigorously and the two were locked in battle when, from outside, there came a mighty roar.

"They're here!" messaged Kai from the rafters.

Simeon backed his way out of the stable, Macki forcing him further and further. As they spilled out into the courtyard, they were greeted by Leonal, Mikel and Pascal, who had climbed over the wall. The head of the mighty Grippon filled the entire archway, the only exit from the courtyard to the lane beyond.

Knowing he was beaten, Simeon let go of his sword and outstretched his hands. His face betrayed no emotion; he was a strategist. He would have to bide his time and wait for another opportunity to present itself.

21

The President

With Simeon's hands firmly bound and Pascal and the Grippon guarding him, Macki, Leonal and Mikel returned to the stable, where they found Julia cupping Aaron's face, as she tried to bring him round from his trance. Leonal felt a pang of jealousy at what looked an intimate moment but pulled himself together. He could see that Aaron was in a state of confusion, seeing the distorted, bloody body of The Illusionist lying amongst the straw of the stable floor. Macki put his arm around Aaron's shoulder and led him outside. Leonal hugged Julia to him and Mikel reached up, patting her on the back to comfort her. She, too, was then guided from the stables.

There was a commotion outside in the lane, as people tried to get by the Grippon. With its head sticking through the archway, it had blocked access to the inn and the rest of the lane. Loud voices could be heard from behind the mammoth beast.

"What is going on here? Make way for the Keepers of Roscar!"

"Let me handle this," said Macki. "Grippon, move aside and let them enter."

The Grippon pulled its head out of the archway, dislodging some of the stonework and sending it crashing to the ground.

"Sorry," it drawled, as everyone looked up, unsure what to make of this creature.

It stepped backwards into the lane, allowing several Keepers of Roscar to enter the courtyard.

"Macki Bond," the leader of the Keepers said, acknowledging that he was acquainted with the Bondsman. "What's going on here? Who are all these people? And why are that man's hands bound?"

"Let's see you get out of this one, Bondsman," Simeon sniggered.

Macki, not to be provoked, ignored Simeon and spoke directly to the leader of the Keepers.

"Vallis Vallier, you know me well enough, I think, to know that I am a man of honour. May we speak privately?"

The leader looked around at the people assembled in the courtyard. He addressed his men, telling them to be on their guard.

"Come with me into the stable. I have something to show you and I will explain all," Macki beckoned to him.

The two men went in and the others stood outside, quietly contemplating what might happen next.

On taking in the dead body, Vallis Vallier exclaimed, "By the gods above! What has been going on here? This had better be good, Macki, or I'll have no choice but to take you all into custody."

Macki told the whole story truthfully, leaving nothing out, even revealing Julia's true identity.

"You know I and many Roscans are sympathetic to your cause," Vallis told him. "But I am charged with keeping Roscar and our people safe. If or when it becomes known that we had helped your cause, the Jahimians would want retribution. I must take this to the President, for as much as I would like to let you all go free, I cannot turn a blind eye to this. You do understand?"

"We will come with you without argument. We will plead our case to your President and hope some solution may be found," answered Macki.

Macki and Vallis returned to the courtyard, and the landlord and patrons of the inn jostled, as they squashed together in the doorway, trying to listen to what was going on. Vallis called to two of his Keepers to follow him into the stables, where he gave orders for them to dispose of The Illusionist's body and clear away all other evidence.

Macki spoke to Julia and her protectors.

"My friends, we must travel with the Keepers to speak with their President in order to complete our journey through Roscar. I have given my word we shall go with them willingly as their guests. I hope you will all cooperate in this. Trust me, my friends, it is for the best."

"We trust in you, Macki. We will do as you say," Julia answered for them all.

"What about me? Untie these bonds!" demanded Simeon. "I am a Jahimian Guardsman sent to take this servant back to the house of General Martinez – where she belongs!"

"I know exactly who you are," Vallis replied, looking Simeon square in the eye. "And you will stay with your hands bound. This is Roscar, not Jahimia, and you have no authority here."

"You will regret this, Keeper," he spat in retort. "Mark my words."

Vallis turned away unperturbed and gave orders for his men and the group of friends to move out. Julia, her band of protectors, Vallis and a dozen of his regimental Keepers, along with Simeon, set off into the darkness of the night and out into the countryside of Roscar.

The weary companions and their Keepers travelled through the night. As dawn broke, they entered a long tree-lined dusty road. In the distance, far away on top of a hill, they saw their first glimpse of the presidential castle. Kai, who had been flying above them, messaged that he would remain on high as he had seen archers on the castle walls.

After continuing on for some time, the road began to ascend the great hill on which the impressive castle stood. Archers strategically aligned the ramparts and the approach was covered in a series of deep ditches which narrowed at the bottom, meaning once you fell in, there was no way out, certainly not without help from above and possibly one or two broken ankles. These ditches ringed the outer walls and the sole access to the castle was via the main road that led up to the three final ditches, which could only be crossed by the lowering of an enormous drawbridge.

An archer dressed in the same green and yellow uniform as that of the Keepers of Roscar called down to them.

"Who goes there? State your names and your reason for being here!"

"I am Vallis Vallier, leader of the Regimental Keepers of Roscar, and with me are twelve of our brothers. We escort Macki Bond and others of his party, who are on a journey through our land. I have brought them here to speak with President Ollisiro for permission to continue on their journey."

"I recognise you, my leader, and also my brother Keepers. Forgive my reticence in admitting you, but I can also see you have a prisoner with his hands tied, a giant of a man and that mammoth creature being ridden by the young boy," he said, falling for Julia's disguise. "What is it?"

"The creature is named Grippon and is not aggressive unless its friends are threatened, one of which is the mountain giant, Pascal. As for the prisoner, he is a Jahimian Guardsman wanted in our land for atrocities carried out some years past," Vallis answered.

"I am what?!" shouted Simeon. "Wanted for atrocities? Are you mad? Do you know who I am?!" he ranted.

"I know exactly who you are. You gave me your name yourself, so there can be no mistake," Vallis answered him, with more than just a hint of disdain. Turning back to look up at the keeper, he called, "Now, enough of this! Open the drawbridge! The prisoner is to be housed in the dungeons."

Slowly, the drawbridge began to descend across the ditches. Once they were inside the outer wall, they were greeted by an open area which housed stables and the fired kiln of a blacksmith's shop, beyond which was a second great wall, with even taller ramparts, which overlooked the first. Vallis led them through an open gated archway. Here, behind the second wall, the castle was coming to life, for it was early in the morning. People going about their business stopped to stare at the strange group of travellers, especially the Grippon and Pascal. Vallis escorted them to a set of stone steps which led up to a solid set of large wooden doors. Two Keepers stood guard.

"My Leader," they both said, by way of greeting.

"I have urgent business with the President. This man," he said, pointing to Macki, "and the young boy will accompany me inside. The rest of their companions are to wait here."

The Keepers, like all who came into contact with the Grippon, stared up at it.

"The creature you see before you is the Grippon. He will do you no harm," Macki informed the men, "but, as Keepers, remember you are charged with upholding the safety of Roscar and its inhabitants, so remain on guard."

He then addressed two of the Keepers who had travelled with them, giving orders for Simeon to be taken to the dungeons and kept under close guard. Simeon scowled, as he was led away.

"You will live to regret this!" he called to Vallis, who ignored him completely and carried on giving orders.

To the rest of his Keepers and the other companions, he gestured to where tables and benches were set out and told them to rest, assuring them that, as his guests, food and drink would be brought to them shortly.

"Come Macki, come child, let us go and speak with President Ollisiro."

They followed Vallis through the heavy wooden doors into a large, cool room with stone floors and a long stone table surrounded by high-backed, cushioned chairs. Sat at the centre of the table, bent over some papers, was an elderly grey-bearded man and beside him, a woman with black corkscrew curls, which fell across her forehead, shading her face from them.

"Wait here!" commanded Vallis. Leaving them at the far end of the room, he made his way over, at which point the woman looked up and stood to greet him.

"President," bowed Vallis. "I beg forgiveness for the intrusion but I have urgent business that I must discuss with you."

"I am sure it is very important. I know you well, Vallis Vallier. You would not have come unannounced had it not been so. Tell me, who are these people that you have brought with you?" she asked.

"It is because of them that I have need to speak with you so urgently, President. Let me explain and then I will bring them forward to meet with you."

President Ollisiro dismissed the elderly gentleman with his paperwork, thanking him and saying they would continue any other business later.

"Come Vallis, sit next to me while you explain. You look like the rest would do you good."

Vallis did as he was bid and told the story exactly as Macki had told it to him.

"You believe him?" Ollisiro asked.

"Yes, I do. The stories of Macki Bond that come out of Jahimia are very different to the ones told by our own people. Roscans tell of his bravery, honesty and compassion," Vallis replied.

"I, too, have heard this. Very well. Bring them forward and I shall speak with them."

Macki and Julia stood before the table. The President got up from her chair. Julia was unable to tell how old the woman before her might be, but her smooth, coffee-coloured skin, deep brown eyes and black hair, which framed her face, made her a very beautiful woman, a fact that Julia noticed was not wasted on Macki.

Macki bowed his head and Julia dipped her knee to curtsy.

"Please sit down," began the President. "You must both be tired from your journey. My Regimental Leader, Vallis Vallier, speaks well of you, Macki Bond. He has told me your story but I would like to hear it from your own lips."

Macki once again told the story from beginning to end, leaving nothing out. Julia listened as he told of her father's murder, of how he had come to this land on the orders of King Joalian of Hamunite, how he and others had been too few to stand up to the army of King Jared of Jahimia and how they had done their best to protect fellow Hamunites, as they travelled here to Roscar. He explained how Julia had escaped when the birthmark had begun to get bigger, and how she had no knowledge of who she was until this time, when her mother could no longer keep it from her. He told of how she had collected many strange companions on her journey and of how they were making their way to Tresgar Tremaine, in the hamlet of Kriel, who had been entrusted with a plan of action by Julia's father should this day come. Finally, he recounted how The Illusionist had kidnapped Julia to hand over to Simeon and of his subsequent accidental death, as she had tried to escape him.

At this point Julia, who had been sitting quietly, let out a small sob. She had stifled the shock of seeing someone die. She had travelled through the night on the warm and comforting back of the Grippon, holding her emotions at bay. Now, hearing the terrible truth aloud, she was engulfed by horror and sorrow. The President came round the table and knelt before her. She reached up and removed the scarf that covered Julia's hair and neck. She lifted her golden-brown curls and felt the back of her neck. Then she enfolded Julia in her arms and stroked the girl's hair while she sobbed and sobbed. When Julia finally settled herself, the President sat down next to her. Taking her hand, she smiled into her face.

"I am Olivia Ollisiro, a commoner elected by the people of Roscar to run this country. You are a girl – no, you are a young woman – who has had to cope with what can only be described as startling revelations, the truth of which is marked out on your neck. It would seem legend is truth and therefore, my dear, you are to be a queen. Fortunately for you, so far, the companions you have gathered seem to have your best interest at heart."

She sighed and turned to Vallis. "Can you order some refreshment for our honoured guests, please? There is much careful thought needed here. I so want to help you but I have need to be wary, for my commitment is to my people and our own land. Eat and rest. I will speak with you both later."

Looking at Macki, she smiled and said, "Julia is indeed lucky to have such dependable companions."

Macki searched her face for a hint of what she might be thinking, but she gave nothing away. She stood to leave, and Macki and Vallis stood also and bowed.

"I will send for you when I have thought through what our next steps will be. You are our guests here but you must remain within the castle walls until such time as we decide what is to be done."

President Ollisiro left the room by a door in the far corner. Macki and Julia joined the rest of their brave and loyal companions and waited.

The further south the companions had gone, the warmer the climate had become. Here inside the castle walls, the heat of the day and the fact they had travelled through the night meant sleep came easily to them. Stretching out to soak up the sunshine, the Grippon filled a substantial space; the rest of the companions found room on benches under the shade of an awning. After some hours of much-needed rest, the travellers started to stir. Macki called them together and explained the situation. Mikel frowned and softly voiced his concerns.

"How long are we to wait and what if what the President decides is not to our liking? Do you have a plan or a solution, Macki?" he asked.

"We need to wait and see what the President has to say, but we need to be on our guard and ready to leave. We will force our way out if needs be. We do not want to make enemies of the Roscans but getting Julia to Hamunite has to be the only thing that matters in the end."

The others listened, their faces showing their concern at the situation they found themselves in. In hushed tones, Leonal, Aaron and Pascal also registered their worries. The Grippon moved closer to Julia. She reached up to stroke it, as it looked at her with sad eyes.

"Don't worry, Grippon, all will be well, I'm sure. Why else would you all have found me, each of you, at my time of need? It is said the ruling of the waves was ordained by the gods when Hamunite and Jahimia became separated, so maybe the gods are looking after us," Julia said, reassuringly.

"Macki!" Vallis called from the steps of the great hall, where they had had their earlier audience with the President. "Come, all of you! The President will speak with you now. Grippon,

Pascal, I am afraid that you will have to wait outside. You will not fit inside the door."

"Something we are used to by now," said Pascal somewhat sadly.

"Okay," the Grippon sighed. It followed the rest of the companions, as they made their way into the hall. It laid his head on its giant paws, its face filling the doorway, as it peered inside.

Keepers of Roscar were stationed around the perimeter of the room. The President stood to greet them. At her side stood a tall, broad man whose dark hair was tinged with grey and a beard that was much the same.

"Tresgar!" Leonal called out in surprise.

The tall man gave a brief smile and nodded to him.

"Your Highness," the President said to Julia, "please be seated, and your companions, too."

The atmosphere in the room was strained. Julia and the others sat themselves down. They glanced at one another wondering what was to come. Macki rested his focus on Tresgar, waiting, watching. Tresgar, in turn, locked eyes with Macki, where they remained until the President began to speak.

"I, along with my advisors, have deliberated long and hard about how to deal with this situation. As I said earlier, I so want to help you, but Roscar must be my prime concern. Therefore, if I allow Julia to renew her journey, I will need some insurance to fall back on should the Jahimians take up arms against us. After all, not only will I have assisted you in your quest, I also have a Jahimian Guardsman of some repute in one of my dungeons."

"So, what do you propose?" Macki asked.

"What I propose is this. Tresgar will take care of everything now. He is, I understand, fully aware of what must be done and was indeed a confidant of Prince Jacob."

Looking Macki straight in the eye, she said, "And you, Macki Bond, will stay here as my insurance. After all, you are the most wanted man in all of Jahimia."

"No!" Julia shouted, jumping to her feet. "I will not have Macki imprisoned here in order for me to go free and make my way to Hamunite."

"Julia, do not distress yourself." Macki placed his hands on her shoulders, turning her to face him. "We have all freely given ourselves to your cause. Your cause is mine and Aaron's also. Remember Hamunite is our home, too. If you do not get there in time and King Joalian dies, we will never set foot in our homeland again and eventually Hamunite will be no more than a desolate island. If this is what it takes to get you home, then I will stay here as security for the President to bargain with. As the President pointed out, Tresgar can take you on from here. Remember, your father trusted him, as did Leonal's father and as do I."

Macki looked once again to Tresgar, who gave a smile of gratitude and nodded in agreement.

Julia looked to Aaron. He nodded rather than speaking. She could sense his distress and looked from one companion to another. In succession, they looked at Macki, then at her and nodded. In the doorway the Grippon let out a small whimper. The President spoke again.

"You will not be locked away, Macki Bond. I trust you to be a man of your word. You shall be my guest here and have the freedom of the castle on the understanding that you agree to remain within our walls. Do I have your word on this?"

"You do, President," Macki answered. "Now, time is of the essence. If you will allow it, my companions need to arrange themselves, and I would like to say my goodbyes."

"Of course. Vallis, let us leave our guests to their business and tell the guards they may leave the room. We will be back shortly to bid you farewell."

After Vallis and the President had gone, Macki and Tresgar embraced.

"I tried to persuade her to allow you to come with us but she was having none of it," Tresgar informed him.

"I know, old friend. All will be well with you to guide them. You understand when you reach the sea surrounding Hamunite, the hawkwings will need to persuade the King to turn the tide and allow you all onto the island."

"So," said Tresgar, turning to Julia, "finally, I get to meet the child who left my home before she could be born. Your Highness, I am your loyal servant."

He bowed his head, then turned to Leonal and embraced him as he had Macki.

Mikel was also known to Tresgar, though they had met in person only once before; that was after Julia's birth, when Tia had contacted him. He, in turn, had travelled to Roscar to pass on the news of Julia's birth and the predicament Isabella and her new baby were in.

Aaron, Tresgar already knew. Along with his father, they would often meet up to discuss how their mutual cause was faring – the safety of Hamunites passing through Jahimia and, most importantly, the day Julia would be ready to make her way to her rightful home on Hamunite.

A small, soft growl reminded them that the Grippon and Pascal were also waiting to be introduced; it lightened the moment and produced a small outburst of laughter.

"Don't worry, Grippon, there is no way you will be forgotten," chuckled Pascal, and sure enough Tresgar came straight out to meet them.

"Are you sure Macki can't come?" the Grippon asked. "I can take him. I climb up and over the walls, you know. I saved Julia."

Macki walked over and stroked the Grippon's side.

"Good friend, I think this time we will have to do as the President asks, but if I am in need of rescue, I will send message with our hawkwing friend and ask him to send you to help me. Speaking of which, where is Kai?"

Kai had hidden himself away in the tree tops which lay to the west of the castle. From there he had tuned into all around him. Young as he was, Kai's telepathic powers were beyond his years. Having been updated by Mikel, he cleared his mind of all else and sent out thought waves to Tia, Fin and any other hawkwing able to pick up his communication.

Tia and Fin, still recuperating at the smallholding, connected with him within minutes. Tia, almost recovered, took charge. Realising how much better she was feeling, Fin sat on the end of the bed, smiling at her indulgently.

"Kai, tell Mikel to double back, cross further up river and head for the home of Lady Alessandra. Fin and I will meet you there. Tresgar may have plans made with Jacob and Macki, but we hawkwings must also have a say in how Julia can best reach Hamunite in safety," Tia ordered.

"What about Macki?" Kai asked.

"Macki will do what is needed – and that is to stay in Roscar as a guest of the President, for now anyway. For Macki, duty will always come first. The others will do what needs to be done also. Don't worry, Kai," Tia answered. "We will see you soon. Keep in touch as you travel."

Back at the castle, the friends all were saying their goodbyes. Julia and Aaron were the most visibly upset. Leonal looked to Macki.

"My friend, what can I say? I wish I had known the truth of you and the Bondsmen sooner. My father was right to trust you, as I do now."

His eyes told the truth in his words and expressed the sadness he felt at leaving Macki behind. Macki shook his hand and slapped his other arm in a gesture of understanding.

"We'll see each other again soon, never fear. You and Aaron mind what Tresgar and Mikel ask of you both. That goes for the hawkwings, too. They only have Hamunite and Julia's welfare at heart. Trust them above all others."

With all the goodbyes done, the band of travellers set off again. Julia had donned her male travelling disguise and she, Mikel,

Leonal, Aaron, Pascal, the Grippon and Tresgar tracked the road away from the castle. Macki watched them from the battlements until they disappeared into the distance. From behind him, President Olivia Ollisiro spoke words of comfort.

"Take heart. You shall see them again."

Without turning to look at her, he gave his answer.

"I know."

22

A Change of Plan

The travellers headed south so as to make sure anyone trailing or watching from the tower would think that was where they were going. The further south they headed, the more tropical, colourful and humid the landscape became. The forest was so dense in parts they had to use their swords to create a path. After an hour or so, on reaching a clearing, Tresgar called them all to a halt.

"It is time to rest and for a change of plan," he said. "We need to follow Tia's orders and head back northwest to Lady Alessandra's home."

The companions congregated in a circle, sharing water and hunks of bread.

"There's something else. We need to set a trail to confuse anyone who may come looking for, or ask after, us."

"Good idea," agreed Mikel.

"I propose Pascal and the Grippon head to my home, as was the original plan, while the rest of us track back northwest. My family will be expecting us all, but I will give you a coded letter. My son, Philippe, will know what to do."

"No!" barked the Grippon. "I won't leave Julia! She need me!"

"Grippon," Pascal intervened, "Julia needs us to do whatever is required to get her to Hamunite, and I understand why you and I should be the ones to do this. Think about it. Which of us are the most conspicuous among our group? You saw the attention we drew at the circus ground. People will talk of us, particularly you, wherever we go. This will make anyone looking for us think Julia and the others could be with us."

The Grippon looked thoughtful, as the rest of the companions awaited its answer. Its head rocked and its jaw jutted out, as it mulled over all Pascal had said.

"We go south, Pascal," it said finally. "We go where we help Julia most."

Julia stood and reached up to stroke the Grippon's ear.

"You are indeed a faithful and loyal friend, Grippon," she said, looking at it fondly.

Tresgar outlined the rest of his plan and then the friends clasped hands in the middle of their circle.

"For Hamunite!" Tresgar called out.

"FOR HAMUNITE!" cried the others in response.

"And for Julia!" Leonal added.

"That goes without saying," Mikel smiled. "Without Julia, there can be no Hamunite, but whether a princess or not, you have captured all our hearts, my dear, and we follow you and your quest as devoted servants."

"No, never as servants," Julia smiled back at them all, "but as my dearest and most loyal friends."

"Okay, okay, enough of the compliments. We must make a move," Tresgar rallied. "Pascal, here is my letter and a small map showing you how to get to Kriel. My home is the large farmhouse with the red-tiled roof. It lies just over the stream. It should not take you much more than half a day. Ask for Philippe and tell him I sent you. He will know what to do."

After saying their goodbyes, Pascal and the Grippon headed south while Julia and the rest of the companions, led by Tresgar, turned northwest. They persisted through the dense forest, creating new pathways. The humidity made them want to drink more but Tresgar, knowing this land, explained they must conserve their water as it would be some hours before they reached a place where they could replenish their flasks.

The going was arduous and slow but finally they came upon a small hamlet with a scattering of wooden and stonebuilt houses and what appeared to be an open-air drinking establishment. Tables and benches had been set in a circle, surrounding a well, on the edge of which sat a large, craggy-faced man. A wide-brimmed green hat sat forward on his head, partly covering his face. Seeing the newcomers, he stood to meet them.

Tresgar dismounted his horse.

"What can I do for you folks?" he asked.

"We'd appreciate filling our flasks," Tresgar answered.

"Well, I can see you're a native Roscan and so you're entitled to a drink from our well, but your friends will need to trade – our water is very precious. This is the only water you'll find round here for miles."

"What sort of thing did you have in mind?" Mikel asked.

By this time other members of the hamlet's community had come to listen to the exchange. The man made a sucking noise and pushed the hat back onto his head.

"Well, it's not often strangers come this way and judging

by the look of you – a dwarf and three young men – you are certainly not from these parts," said the man, deceived by Julia's disguise. "How about you sit down and share a story or two with us? We don't get much news from the outside world, you know," he added with a smile.

A woman came forward. "Yes, please join us. I have some pineapple and mango you can share," she offered.

Tresgar turned to his companions. "Come, let us join these kind people!" he declared. As the others dismounted, Tresgar put an arm around Leonal and Aaron's shoulders. "Keep your eyes and ears open," he whispered to them, before patting them on the back and stepping forward to accept a drink. He smiled and nodded to the rest of the people of the hamlet.

Leonal and Aaron flanked Julia, and Mikel followed them to the tables, where they all sat down. The man in the hat gave them all a cup of water then leaned forward, resting his hands on the table.

"So then, who's going to tell us about themselves first?" he asked, though it felt more like a demand than a question.

23

Kriel

The Grippon and Pascal made good time. The heat of the day was upon them, yet they did not break stride and walked on with purpose and determination. The sooner we get there and deliver Tresgar's letter, the sooner we can get back to our friends, Pascal had told Grippon. This was all the incentive needed to keep on going as quickly as possible.

Passing through a small village, they attracted stares and gasps and cries of "Giants!" The countryside became more open and hilly. The dusty roads they trod upon added to their thirst and soon their water was all gone. Standing on the top of a hill above a second, larger, village, Pascal pointed to a stream.

"Let's go round the village so we can fill our flasks."

"We not supposed to be seen. People supposed to think Julia come this way," drawled the Grippon.

"Well, I shouldn't worry too much about that. Judging by the amount of people that have come out onto the road to gawp at us, I'd say we've already been spotted," Pascal grinned, striding on down the hill, towards the stream.

Children were playing in the water.

The Grippon and Pascal drew nearer. The sight of the giant man and dog-like creature descending on them sent the children screaming.

"Don't be afraid!" Pascal shouted to them. "We won't hurt you!"

One little child fell over, banging his head on a small rock. The Grippon bounded forward, picked him up in its mouth and deposited him on the ground. As the Grippon lifted its head, an arrow caught it just above its eye – followed by more arrows, most just bouncing off him.

"Stop!" cried Pascal.

"Yes, stop!" bawled the Grippon. "Boy need help!"

The people lowered their bows in amazement.

"It talks!" one of them yelled to the others. "I've never seen anything like it in all my life!"

"Well, of course you haven't!" shouted Pascal. "He's one of a kind. Now, stop messing about and help the child."

A woman, who turned out to be the boy's mother, ran forward. The boy, by this time, was beginning to recover. Forcing his way out of his mother's embrace, he sat up and stared at the Grippon; a small trickle of blood, where he had hurt his head, running down his face.

"I was in your mouth," the boy stated.

"Yes," confirmed the Grippon.

"But you didn't hurt me. You were gentle," he said, astounded.

"We don't hurt anyone. We only want some water."

"Yes, that's all we want and then we'll be on our way," Pascal explained.

The villagers apologised for their behaviour and by the time Pascal and the Grippon had drunk their fill and replenished their flasks, the villagers were sorry to see them go. They waved goodbye and went on their way.

Within the hour, they had arrived at their destination. The large farmhouse was just as Tresgar had described it. The red-tiled roof glimmered in the late afternoon sunlight, as they made their way into the farmyard. Even though it was large, the Grippon and Pascal took up a great deal of space. All seemed quiet – the gentle hum of bees; the mooing of dairy cattle sheltering from the heat of the afternoon under a cluster of trees.

"Stay prepared, Grippon. We don't know who is around or who could be watching," Pascal said, before knocking gently on the farmhouse door with his large knuckles.

"Hello," he called. "I am looking for Philippe Tremaine."

Slowly, the door opened and a younger version of Tresgar stepped out. He pulled the door closed behind him and looked up, taking in the size of the man before him. His eyes grew even wider when he saw the size of the furry animal lying on the great stone flags of the farmyard floor.

"Who are you and what is your business here?" the young man asked.

"Well, I should say, looking at you, you are Philippe Tremaine – and if that is so, I have a message from your father," Pascal smiled down at him.

"From my father?"

Pascal held out the message from Tresgar, but as the man reached out to take it, Pascal bent to look him in the eye.

"You are Philippe?" he asked, wanting to be sure.

"If you have met my father, do you doubt it?" the young man grinned.

Smiling back at him, Pascal released his grip, allowing Philippe to take the message.

24

Tall Tales

The companions seated themselves on the benches that surrounded the well. Leonal and Aaron sat either side of Julia while Tresgar positioned himself next to the weathered man with the green hat. Mikel drew attention to himself by standing on the horse's back, then tumbling forwards and jumping up onto the bench directly opposite where Tresgar and the man were sat.

"I shall regale you with the tale of our journey so far," Mikel began, drawing on his experience as an entertainer. With one hand up, the other holding his hat to his chest, he took a deep bow.

The woman who had offered the fruit returned carrying a platter of delicious-looking pineapple and mango.

"Here you are, my dears," she said in an almost overly cheerful manner.

As she spoke, Aaron noticed a cloud of dust to the rear of the dwelling, where the woman had just come from. He and Leonal both heard the distant drum of horses' hooves. Their eyes met for a brief moment, both aware that there was something more than just the offer of drinks in exchange for tales happening here.

"Tell your tale then, little man," the green-hatted man said.

Mikel began by recounting his circus days and how he had recently been performing on the outskirts of Tovey. He even told them how a few nights ago he had drunk rather too much ale and had ended up asleep under a table in a bar and had woken the next day to find the circus packed up and gone. He was a gifted storyteller and soon had the people of the hamlet hanging on his every word.

"So what did you do?" a young boy in the audience asked.

"Well, I had no money left and had no idea which way they had gone. I was beside myself. My foolish weakness for the ale had, alas, left me in a real quandary. Then, as luck would have it, this fine Roscan," Mikel gestured to Tresgar, "took pity on me and gave me the chance to join him and his companions here, who he had just taken on as extra hands to help with his harvest."

"So," said the rugged-faced man, "you're a farmer, are you?" He directed this question straight at Tresgar.

"Yes, that is correct," Tresgar replied, maintaining eye contact.

"Whereabouts would your farm be?" the man said, continuing his interrogation.

"My farm is to the south but we are travelling northwest first, where I have secured the purchase of some new and much-needed farming tools."

"So, on your travels, have you come across any unusual characters?"

"When you travel as widely as I do with the circus," Mikel answered, "it makes a change to meet people who are not unusual!" He was still acting the entertainer, elaborating each word and spreading his arms wide. "It has been a nice change for me to meet up with this fine farmer and his workforce."

"Mikel here has helped keep our hearts light, as we have travelled, regaling us with his circus stories."

"Then, I wonder," interjected the man, "if you know of the latest rumours we are hearing of a giant with a great big dog travelling with the circus, and the death of a magician?"

"What?!" gasped Mikel. "I was surely not intoxicated for so long that such things could have occurred without me knowing or me having some inkling of a memory!"

"Well," the man sighed, "we are a poor village and the Jahimians are hunting the companions of the giant and his dog. The rewards for information would be great."

Tresgar stood legs astride, hands spread on the table.

"Well, we thank you for your hospitality, but as for any information on a giant and a dog, however large, we haven't seen or heard anything regarding this strange rumour."

Julia, Leonal and Aaron had all sat silently throughout; they had exchanged glances but nothing more. Aaron suspected that the dust cloud he'd seen earlier was made by a horse and rider, perhaps sent to inform on strangers arriving at the village. There was no way he could pass this on to his companions without causing suspicion, though.

"Okay, sir," Leonal said, turning to speak directly to Tresgar. "What would you have us do now?"

"I think we will get ourselves together and be on our way," declared Tresgar.

"Now then," began the man, "don't be so hasty. Nightfall is on its way and there are no other places to stop over between here and the river. Here, we can offer you shelter and supplies for the rest of your journey. The forest can be a strange and uncomfortable place to spend the night."

"It must be said that you seem very keen to keep us here," Tresgar replied. "I wonder what advantage there is for you."

"I assume if you have money for tools, you would also be able to pay for provisions and a place to stay? The well and our homegrown produce are really the only way of earning a living for the residents of the hamlet."

Suddenly the thunder of horses' hooves came rumbling towards them. Three riders entered the village centre. One jumped straight down and made his way to the man with the rough face.

"Grandfather, the General has sent two of his men to check out our visitors," said the rider, taking off his hat. It was clear to see he was no more than a gangly lad of about twelve or thirteen. Tresgar stood tall.

"What is the meaning of this?!"

The other two riders, dressed in Jahimian guard uniforms, turned to look at him.

"We are searching for a member of General Martinez of Jahimia's household who has disappeared and been reported to be in this area. She was last seen around the time some trouble took place at the circus. This coincided with the reports of a giant and a gigantic dog. We think they may be travelling together."

Mikel tumbled from the table down in front of the Guardsmen.

"Do you see any giants here? I think it's fair to say that none of our party fit the description of 'giant', would you agree?"

However, rather than agree, the Guardsman pursued.

"The person who has disappeared is of Hamunite appearance, and I think you'll agree that at least two members of your party have such colouring."

Tresgar took a deep breath and drew himself up to his full height. He laid his right hand on the hilt of his sword and nodded to Leonal and Aaron.

"I think, gentlemen, you are off track. You are currently in the land of Roscar, where Jahimian guards have no authority. Also, unlike Jahimians, Roscans have no problem treating Hamunites as equals. Well, most Roscans, that is."

Tresgar made this last remark while making a point of glaring at the weather-beaten man. "Come on, boys," he commanded, "get the horses and we will be on our way."

Dipping his hand into his pocket, Tresgar drew out some coins; he selected two and laid them on the table. "That should cover the cost of the food and water, although water is a natural resource and belongs to all."

The companions began to make their way to their horses; Leonal and Aaron still flanking Julia, with Tresgar and Mikel bringing up the rear guard.

Meanwhile, a heated discussion had broken out at the well between the residents and the Jahimian Guardsmen. The companions ignored it, mounted their horses and left the way they had come.

"Where are we going, Tresgar?" Leonal asked.

"I spotted a clearing about a ten-minute ride before we got to that village. It will be safer there just for this one night, I think," Tresgar replied.

All companions were in agreement and rode on.

❖

They arrived at the clearing and quickly set up camp. They settled down for the night, with Aaron assigned to take first watch.

"Wake me if you hear anything even slightly unusual or worrying," Tresgar ordered.

Leonal and Julia lay side by side at the trunk of a large tree.

"Julia, how are you doing?" asked Leonal.

"Honestly, I am fine," said Julia. "I am not worried for myself, for I have the most wonderful friends taking care of me. However, my concern for my mother grows, as time goes by, especially now I know that General Martinez is actively looking for me here in Roscar."

"He is a bold one, that's for sure," answered Leonal.

"Bold, arrogant and ruthless," she replied. "He has been waiting for his chance to invade Hamunite since the day I was born, if what my mother and Mikel have told me is true."

Overhearing the conversation, Mikel piped up.

"True? Of course it's true. What other reason could all of us have for roaming around the Roscan countryside?"

"Okay everyone, settle down now and, please, stay prepared," commanded Tresgar.

Aaron was just in the process of waking Leonal to take over his watch when the shadow of a man appeared behind the trees. Aaron placed his hand over Leonal's mouth, as he gently shook him awake. Aaron pointed towards the shadow and removed his hand from Leonal's mouth.

"I will wake Tresgar," he said in a whisper, "then you take the right side and I will take the left. We will capture whoever is there in a pincer movement."

Leonal agreed and Aaron woke Tresgar. The older man heard the plan and quickly agreed, with a warning to be careful. As they reached the shadow, they were ready to seize the intruder, when he stepped forward into the clearing.

"A very good morning to you all," he declared, removing his hood. The companions gasped in pleasure at the sight of Macki Bond. Kneeling down beside Julia, he took her hand in his.

"I do hope you have been well looked after in my absence, Princess?" he said.

"Father!" Aaron called, rushing forward to hug Macki. The rest of the companions welcomed him with handshakes and backslapping. Then Julia voiced what they were all thinking.

"But Macki, how did you get here? How did you escape from the presidential castle?"

"Well, if we settle down, I have some supplies. A breakfast of fruit, bread and tea for all while I tell my story, I think," Macki responded.

"About half a day after you left, President Ollisiro received a small band of visitors led by General Martinez. She and I were having dinner at the time but she didn't hesitate and ordered the General to be brought before her. I wish you could have seen the look on his face when he saw me sitting there at the table in the big hall, eating dinner with the President."

Macki could not help grinning from ear to ear, as he told his story.

"General Martinez came in blustering and demanding to know what the President was doing sitting down to dinner with such a wanted criminal. Olivia Ollisiro told him in no uncertain terms that he had better choose his words carefully or he might find himself incarcerated with his man servant in one of her dungeons!" laughed Macki.

"And how dare he presume to tell her what she should or should not do in her own country. Then she went on to ask him if he had entered Roscar on orders from King Jared. He admitted he had not and began to tell a story of a servant girl who had run away from his household. Martinez then accused me and my fellow Hamunites who reside in Roscar of aiding and abetting this servant in her flight. Olivia reminded him that he had no right to make accusations about anyone in Roscar and told him that first thing the next morning she would have the General, his men and Simeon escorted off Roscan soil, with the warning that should he return again without permission, she would take this as an act of war and would advise King Jared of the intrusion forthwith."

Macki took a swig of tea through smiling lips before continuing with his tale.

"True to her word, she released Simeon and sent General Martinez and his men on their way first thing the next morning. Accompanied by Vallis Vallier and his men, they were escorted to the nearest crossing back to Jahimia. However, I am led to understand that the impudent Martinez returned as soon as Vallis turned his back on them, for they have recently been seen in these very woods, according to a young Roscan girl who sold me the fruit and bread."

"A heart-warming tale, Macki, I think we can all agree," Tresgar stated with a raised eyebrow, "yet it doesn't include how it came to be that the President released you."

"Well, it seems that Martinez's bare-faced cheek at entering Roscar without permission meant I was no longer needed as a bargaining tool. Also, I think it fair to say that, by the time of the General's little visit, President Ollisiro had warmed to me anyway," said Macki with a grin, "for as she kissed me goodbye, she told me that I would always be a welcome visitor at the castle."

"Are you serious, Father?" asked Aaron. "You and the President of Roscar?"

"Don't knock it, Son," he winked. "It pays to have friends in high places."

At this, the companions all broke into laughter.

25

Triorey

The mood in the camp felt considerably lighter with Macki's return, though while Tresgar had enjoyed his friend's tale of the President and the General, he was beginning to feel anxious about the amount of time they had now spent catching up.

"Right, come on everyone, we need to get going," he declared. "At this rate, Philippe and our rather conspicuous companions will arrive at the meeting point way ahead of us."

"Yes, yes, indeed time is pressing," Mikel agreed, "but has anyone heard from Kai recently?"

"No, there has been nothing since we left the castle," Julia answered.

"Okay," frowned Mikel, "let's move on but as we do, open your minds to Kai and try to reach him."

Suddenly, a voice came to them all.

"Well, hello everybody! You've finally decided you've missed me. And Macki, it is wonderful to hear your thoughts again and know you are back with us. I have been here all the time, flying high above and keeping an eye on proceedings. I have informed Tia and Fin of the latest developments. She is happy to keep on track and all meet up at Lady Alessandra's home, as planned. Donald is escorting them all the way, along with another of your Bondsmen, named Rob."

"Well, knowing that Donald and Rob will be adding to our numbers is reassuring," Macki answered.

Tia rested peacefully amongst the cushions of the wagon provided by the De Silvas, with Fin at her side and Donald and Rob riding up front. Rob had answered Fin's call for help from any Hamunites in the area. He was one of the men who had tackled Simeon and his Guardsmen in the mountain pass. Having become a Bondsman some three years ago due to lack of prospects on Hamunite itself, he had come in search of Macki and his men and been welcomed by his fellow self-exiled Hamunites. Now, the excitement he felt at being part of these new developments – a chance to go home and visit his mother and brother, and to be a part of bringing their future queen home – filled him with hope and pride. As well as this, he had, since childhood, long been fascinated by the hawkwing colony, knowing how clever, kind and caring they were and the valuable part they played in Hamunite itself. So, for all of this, along with the camaraderie with his fellow Bondsmen, he had jumped at the chance to become involved in such an important mission.

Back in Kriel, things had developed at quite some pace. Philippe had been down to the harbour and negotiated the passage for himself, Pascal and the Grippon. They made a deal with the captain of an enormous sailing ship with ample room for the two colossal friends. The captain's name was Maurice Mariner, a seaman who had spent nearly his whole life on deck. He was not at all fazed by the size of the giant, or indeed the beast. Philippe added that the pair were strong swimmers and would manage going overboard in an emergency.

What did worry Maurice was the next part of the plan, which was to pick up the rest of the companions and sail them to Hamunite. With Philippe's assurance that the tide would be turned, the Roscan captain found courage in the promise of such an adventure and the faith he had in the Tremaine family, whom he had known for most of his time in Kriel. He agreed a price and they set sail that very evening.

The party from Kriel said their goodbyes to the locals. Philippe's mother, Florence, and his sisters, Helena and Theresa, told them to keep safe and to look out for their father.

Julia's group of companions now too were on their way and making good time. By nightfall, they were almost at the river estuary which they needed to follow in order to reach the harbour, one mile from Triorey, where the ship would dock, ready for the next leg of their journey.

"Where can we cross safely?" Julia asked.

"Do not worry, Princess. All is in hand. There is another ferry crossing which we can take. If it still runs to time, on the hour, as it always has, it will take us and the horses all the way into the harbour," answered Tresgar.

So, they tracked the river down to the mouth of the estuary, where they found, as if waiting by order, the large ferry. The ferryman, a young, well-built Jahimian, and his companion of similar size, heaved their heavy load up the estuary and, in what seemed like no time at all, they reached the harbour of Triorey. They docked at the designated space for the ferry and soon got off. Macki warned everyone that they were now back on Jahimian soil and therefore must be on their guard and be careful what they said to anyone showing any kind of interest in them. The dock housed the large sail ship which had recently brought the others from Kriel.

Under Mikel's orders, Kai had been trying to message Pascal, Grippon and Philippe. When he finally got through, Pascal informed him they were already making their way to Lady Alessandra's as they thought it unwise to hang around the harbour, looking so conspicuous.

"Quite right, too," Mikel agreed, when Kai shared this information with him.

Adhering further orders from Mikel, the hawkwing messaged Pascal.

"We will meet you at Lady Alessandra's. I believe Tia, Fin, Donald and Rob are already there. We'll see you all soon."

Everyone began to feel a little more hopeful that they were going to be able to see this mission through to its conclusion.

Although she felt much happier at their prospects, Julia was nervous about meeting her grandmother for the first time. Having lived at Lady Alessandra's mansion as a child, Mikel knew his way around Triorey and so he took the lead, with the rest of the companions following close behind. Julia made her way to the front until she was riding side by side with him.

"I am very nervous, Mikel. Will she like me, do you think?" she asked him.

"Like you? She will love you! Imagine having known for

sixteen years you have a grandchild that you have been denied seeing when, suddenly, one day, there she is before you; a real, living, beautiful young woman. You have absolutely nothing to fear from your grandmother. Lady Alessandra is kind and caring. Fortunately, your mother takes after her – and not your selfish grandfather."

Then, excitedly, Mikel shouted out, "Look! There ahead! Can you see the rooftops of the mansion?"

Indeed, they all could, but what they hadn't seen or heard was the band of Jahimian Guardsmen, who had positioned themselves a few metres from the gates of the carriageway leading up to the house.

"Halt! Who goes there?" came a shout.

"Leave this to me," Mikel said, before adding, "Kai, try and reach Tia and Fin and relay what is happening."

The hawkwing quickly responded that he would do so.

"Good evening, gentlemen," Mikel addressed the Guardsman. "Has something happened?"

The Guardsman in charge stood before Mikel, rising to his full height.

"Why would you think something had happened?" he asked.

"Well, seeing a band of Guardsmen on the open road this late in the evening is somewhat unusual, unless you have been called to deal with a situation of some kind," Mikel answered.

Macki and Tresgar nodded to each other and then to Leonal and Aaron, indicating that they were ready. Indeed, they did need to be ready, for just then, the leader of the Guardsmen gave orders to his men to draw their swords and let no one through.

"How dare you refuse entry to my guests!" came an authoritative voice from behind the Guardsmen.

Sitting astride the Grippon was Lady Alessandra. She commanded the Guardsmen to put away their swords and allow the companions through.

"My Lady, we are under orders from General Martinez to allow no one entry to your property," protested the leader of the Guardsmen.

"General Martinez is already being sought by King Jared for taking it upon himself to give orders and sanction missions without permission of the King," she replied, curtly. "And as you rightly say, this is my property, my land, and I will decide who is welcome here."

The companions, their hands on the hilts of their swords, looked on.

Tresgar addressed the Jahimian leader.

"I am Tresgar Tremaine, former master of the castle guards of Jahimia and I think you should sheath your weapons and do as My Lady says. This is not the way of Guardsmen, certainly not in my day."

It was quiet for some time, though the Guardsmen were visibly processing the information they had been given.

"But what are you doing here?" their leader asked.

"That is none of your business," Lady Alessandra countered.

The rest of the Guardsmen began muttering amongst themselves before another decided to take charge.

"Stand down! Allow My Lady's visitors through!" he ordered. "We know not what the General has based this mission upon and if he is even still in charge. Let us retreat to the castle and try to ascertain what this business is all about."

"Ah, so there is at least one among you with some form of sense," Lady Alessandra said, before turning to the companions. "Now, come, my friends. Welcome to my home."

The Guardsmen dispersed and the companions followed the Grippon, as it carried Lady Alessandra through the gates and up the long, winding carriageway. On reaching the house, they found Pascal and Philippe waiting for them by the grand doorway that led on into the mansion's grand hall. Up on the second floor, Donald and Rob were stationed at the windows, with bows and arrows at the ready.

Everyone hugged and to their delight Tia and Fin suddenly appeared. Kai flew to greet them.

"Amazing! You are flying again!" he gasped.

Julia and Lady Alessandra stared at each other until, finally, Lady Alessandra took hold of her granddaughter's hands and asked her to join her in the great hall, where she enveloped her in a tender embrace.

"Oh, my darling girl, I have prayed for this day. Only, I had hoped your mother would be with us, too."

Unable to contain her emotions any longer, the sobbing came, racking Julia's body.

"How I wish she were here, too. Is there any word of my mother?" Julia asked.

"Fin has been contacting people all over the land and it would appear that the King has now discovered what General Martinez has been up to and is none too happy about it. Unbelievably, King Jared had no idea that you and Isabella had been held captive all these years. He summoned General Martinez to ask him to explain himself but the General, by this time, had taken it upon himself to follow Simeon into Roscar, leaving Isabella behind. The King sent for her to become a guest once more in his own castle fortress. She is safe and well and has been able to communicate with Fin and Tia. She has agreed to stay in the protection of King Jared until you are safely delivered home to Hamunite and the problem of General Martinez has been resolved."

"But King Jared," said Julia fearfully, "he was angry with Mamma. He wanted to marry her when she ran off with Father. She will not be safe with him."

"He did wish to marry Isabella, it is true," Lady Alessandra said, "but that was many years ago and the King is not the man he was. It has brought him great sorrow and regret to know the part he inadvertently played in your father's death and the countless other atrocities that General Martinez has committed in his name, most of which have only very recently come to light. No, my dear, far from wanting Isabella for his bride, it seems that King Jared now looks at her in the way he always should have – as a friend to his own daughter, Jasmina, and as a respected Lady of the King's Court."

"Oh my goodness," Julia weeped, in disbelief, "Mamma is safe!"

More tears flowed, as the rest of the companions made their way into the great hall through a doorway so large that even the Grippon was able to squeeze through. Once they were inside, the story was relayed to them all.

Following a moving reunion with his father, Philippe was introduced to the remaining members of the group. Tresgar asked where Maurice Mariner, the captain of the ship, was.

"He has stayed aboard with his crew, Father," Philippe explained. "He said that he would have to fill in docking paperwork but will be ready to sail at first light."

"Well then, my friends, we need to settle down and rest, for tomorrow will be a long and emotional day."

Most were shown to bedrooms but the Grippon and Pascal had to make do with a night's rest in the great hall. However, since they were so used to sleeping in the wild, this still seemed somewhat of a luxury. Meanwhile, Lady Alessandra took Julia upstairs to a bedroom of her own. Macki followed them and remained on guard outside. Lady Alessandra thanked him for his diligence.

Leonal told Macki that should tiredness overcome him, he would be quite ready to relieve him. Lady Alessandra noticed the shy smiles shared between Julia and Leonal, and nodded. They all said their goodnights and turned in for some much-needed sleep.

Everyone was up before dawn, preparing for their departure; the atmosphere a mixture of excitement and trepidation. Macki and Tresgar called them together in the great hall. Tresgar spoke first.

"In order for this plan to work, we must all be vigilant and cooperate fully. Pascal and Grippon, we may have to ask you to undertake a dangerous swim amongst the tides."

"The tide may not be the only problem, though," Macki interjected. "A sea serpent dwells in the deep waters surrounding Hamunite. If it is disturbed, it may spell trouble for ones even as mighty as the two of you."

Pascal patted the Grippon's side at these words.

"We have come this far," Pascal said. "We will not let you down. Julia has indicated that she will champion our cause to become part of the Hamunite community and no longer have to hide."

There was a look of longing in the giant's eye as he said this. "More importantly, our love for Julia and the wish to help her complete this quest is incentive enough."

"Grippon and Pascal love Julia," drawled the Grippon.

Tears rolled down Julia's face. She stroked the Grippon and touched Pascal's arm in a gesture of thanks.

The time had come for the final leg of the journey. In small groups, the companions made their way to the harbour and the awaiting ship. The Tremaines led the party, being the only ones previously known to the captain. Macki, Aaron, Rob and Leonal formed a guard to lead Julia to the ship. Mikel and Donald escorted Lady Alessandra, while Pascal and Grippon brought up the rear. The three hawkwings hovered over the groups, ready to message about any problems that might occur.

Everyone aboard, the ship lay very low in the water. The weight of the passengers meant that the cast-off wasn't the easiest of Maurice Mariner's years at sea, but the strong and experienced captain slowly but surely guided the great ship out of the harbour and into open water, finally setting sail for Hamunite.

26

The Seas of Hamunite

After a fairly rough start, the ship moved into deeper water and the journey became smoother. For some time, the voyage felt almost peaceful. The bright sunshine caused the water around them to glisten, as the shape of the island of Hamunite came into view on the horizon. However, this feeling of contentment was not to last long.

Waves soon began forming around them, small at first but swiftly growing greater in size until, for all the beauty ahead, the water became evermore treacherous. The ship was now beginning to roll violently on the tides and Macki knew it was time to take action. He saw Lady Alessandra sat on a bench that had been secured to the deck. He caught Tresgar's eye and indicated towards Julia's grandmother. Understanding immediately, the Roscan made his way to her.

"My Lady," he said, "the seas are becoming more than a little choppy, I fear. Would you allow my son to escort you below deck, where you may be a little more comfortable?"

"What a polite way of saying that you don't want an old woman on deck," she replied sternly.

"My Lady, I meant no offence," Tresgar began to explain. "I only meant—"

"I know very well what you meant," said Lady Alessandra with a wry smile, "but fear not, Tresgar, I may be rather stubborn but I am certainly not stupid. The last thing you need on these seas is to be worrying about me being swept overboard. Just make sure that fate does not come to my granddaughter."

"Of course, My Lady. Julia's safety is paramount."

"Indeed," she said, looking across at the young girl. "Keep her safe and she will take care of the rest of us."

Tresgar found these words curious but there was no time to ponder. He called to Philippe and instructed him to escort Lady Alessandra below deck. Philippe looked at his father in a manner that suggested that he would much rather stay above deck with the other young men, but he knew duty always came first.

"Do not worry," Lady Alessandra said to the younger Tremaine, "I shall keep you safe."

"Thank you, My Lady," smiled Philippe, offering her his arm. "I very much appreciate it."

"You're a fine young man," she said, taking his arm, as they made their way below.

Macki was forging ahead with the plan and had begun making arrangements for their safety with the hawkwings.

"Tia, how are your injuries?" he asked. "Are you able to fly far?"

"Yes, I'm fine," she said, though Fin gave her a look that suggested he wasn't so sure.

"Good," said Macki. "We need you to fly ahead and speak with King Joalian. Explain the whole story and ask him – beg if you must – to turn the tide."

"Of course," she said without hesitation and immediately set off towards the island.

Fin was as concerned for her as ever but knew that she would always put duty first, so he took to the air himself and within moments was by her side, flying on to Hamunite. Looking over his shoulder, he saw the ship rolling evermore desperately on the seas.

The ship rocked hard and each time it lurched, gallons of water came on board, soaking them all. Maurice shouted instructions.

"Hold fast onto the side ropes! Wrap them around your wrists!" he bellowed. "Tresgar, if we carry on with this much weight, we are sure to capsize. I think it's time for our friends to go for a swim."

"No!" shouted Julia. "It's too dangerous!"

"But Julia," Pascal implored, "if we do not do this thing, we may all perish. We have agreed to it freely, come what may."

"I ready, Pascal," drawled the Grippon, "though if there time for one more hug from Julia, I go happier."

Julia quickly bounded across the deck, just as the next wave smashed over the side. She was swept along, certain to be flung overboard, when suddenly the Grippon had her in its mouth. As the ship steadied, it placed her in Leonal's open arms and without another word, leapt into the sea.

"Farewell, my friends, and good luck!" shouted Pascal. "I hope that we shall meet again on the shore."

Then he dived in, to join his friend in the raging sea.

Tia and Fin reached King Joalian's hilltop fortress. They asked for a meeting, stressing that the future of Hamunite was at stake, and were promptly hurried into King Joalian's chambers. They found an aged, fragile man in his bed, supported by plumped-up pillows and cushions. The ravages of time were plain to see on his drawn face, but there was something more than that. The air of sorrow around this decrepit old man wasn't necessarily something that could be seen, but it could certainly be felt.

Looking at King Joalian, Tia hoped the news they were about to share with him would not cause his condition to deteriorate further, but share they must, for the lives of their friends and indeed the future of Hamunite depended on it.

"Your Majesty," began Tia, telepathically, "the hour is late and the situation is grave."

Julia and the others had followed Maurice's orders and were holding on for dear life. The vessel continued to clash against the waves, lunging violently from side to side, as the winds tore at them. As deeply as it hurt Julia to see the Grippon and Pascal go overboard, and as hard as she had protested against the necessity of their selfless act, she had to concede that the captain had been right. Had they still been carrying their colossal weight, the ship would surely have overturned.

Everyone was clinging to ropes apart from Maurice, who had tied a line about his waist in order to keep his hands free to grasp the ship's wheel. His powerful, sinewy arms worked tirelessly to keep them upright, with a strength that belied his years. Julia was astonished at how he was managing to grapple with the elements so fiercely but was at the same time troubled – surely the old seaman could not endure such a punishing endeavour for long. She quickly found out that she was not alone in her concerns, on hearing Tresgar, who was clenching a rope not far from her, call out to the captain.

"Maurice!" yelled the Roscan. "How much longer can we withstand such a beating?"

"You always were a land lover, Tresgar!" joked Maurice, with an almost maniacal look in his eye. "As much as I would love to tell you that it's just a bit of weather, truly, in all my years, I have never known seas as brutal as this. I fear if they keep at us as they are, we have no more than a matter of minutes before this old ship is torn to pieces!"

It was imperative that Tia and Fin got the King to turn the tide soon, or not only would their mission fail at the last, but indeed they would all lose their lives, including the heir to the throne of Hamunite. Tresgar called out to Kai, in the hope that the young hawkwing was still with them.

"Kai, are you there?"

"I am still with you, yes," returned the voice of the hawkwing. "I have managed to stay above the worst of the weather and follow you, Tresgar. Things look pretty desperate down there."

"Indeed, they are," replied the Roscan. "We haven't much time, Kai. You need to contact Tia and Fin and urge them to hurry. Maurice knows the seas as well as any man alive and he says that we won't last more than a few minutes unless the King turns the tide."

"I understand," said Kai, before breaking off from Tresgar. The young hawkwing then focused all of his abilities on reaching out to Tia and Fin, on the island.

Even telepathically, recounting all that had happened, starting with the circumstances of Jacob's death and Julia's birth, right up to them leaving Triorey and setting off from the harbour, had taken almost an hour. Tia knew that their time was short but also that she must tell the King everything, for if he did not believe the truth of the tale, then he would surely not agree to turn the tide for them.

As Tia relayed their account, Fin hovered by the great window of King Joalian's chambers, anxiously looking out to sea. Far in the distance, he could just make out the ship. It looked no more than a toy, but even from here, Fin could see that their friends were not faring well. Indeed, the ship disappeared from view every so often. Each time, Fin's heart sank to the pit of his stomach until the vessel reappeared on the horizon.

Despite his weariness the King exerted all his effort to receive Tia's message and listened intently. There were moments when Tia could not be sure if Joalian was still conscious, but then he would groan in distress at the injustices the companions, especially Julia, had suffered, so Tia then knew he had heard it all.

"And now, Your Highness," she pressed on, "your granddaughter is out there upon the sea, making her way to you, but she and her friends are in dire need of your help. The tides are ferocious and our friends Pascal and the Grippon have already risked their lives to keep Julia safe, though I fear it will not be enough. We need you to turn the tide so that they can make it safely to Hamunite, or they will be lost to the sea."

King Joalian wept inconsolably. He seemed like a child now, so small and weak had he become. Just then, Tia and Fin looked at each other: Kai's voice had come into their minds as clearly as though he was in the room with them.

"Tia, Fin, can you hear me!"

Tia maintained her contact with the King while Fin replied, "Yes, Kai, we can hear you. You are still some distance away from us but the ship doesn't look to be holding up too well from here."

"It is worse than that, Fin," conveyed the younger hawkwing. "The captain says it will only be a matter of moments before the ship is torn asunder."

Hearing this, Tia spoke again to King Joalian and implored him to intervene.

"Your Majesty, please!" she pleaded, crying. "Julia needs you. Her friends need you. Hamunite needs you. Please, Your Majesty, you must turn the tide or everything will be lost!"

The King sobbed and shuddered. Tia was not sure that he had even heard the last of what she had said when, suddenly, without warning, he broke from his reverie and sat up. The hawkwings heard his voice bellow with a ferocity that one so frail did not seem capable of.

"I call upon the gods to turn the tide! Allow safe passage to the ship sailing our seas and all of the souls aboard. Let the waters calm in their favour and see them safely to our harbour!"

Without a further word, the King collapsed upon his bed.

Julia was not sure how much longer she could hold onto the rigging. She did not have the brute strength of their captain to keep herself in place, let alone to keep the ship upright in the astounding manner he had. Try as she might to maintain a grip, her fingers slipped on the wet rope. The ship hit a gigantic wave, forcing its bow skyward, until, finally, she could hold on no more. Her arms and legs flailed in desperation, as she plummeted towards her doom. Just then, she felt her arm jolt. Instead of falling she was now swinging through the air. Julia looked up to see Leonal with one arm clinging to a rope and the other clasping her wrist.

"I think that this is not the best time for you to be going swimming," he said with a smile, which quickly turned to a grimace as he held her, suspended in the air. "Now, just you hold on, you hear me? Don't you let go."

The ship smacked back down, and Julia with it. She bashed her knees on the deck before being hurtled in the opposite direction, as the next wave collided. She clung to Leonal for dear life. He maintained his grip as best he could, but Julia knew in her heart that they would not have the strength to hold through the next wave. She looked into Leonal's eyes and said a silent goodbye, as she felt herself falling, for the final time. Sure enough, they lost their grip. She saw the look of terror in his face, as they were torn apart. She closed her eyes and braced herself for the impact of the water – but it never came.

Instead, she slid across the wet surface of the deck and came to a natural stop. She opened her eyes and looked up to see Leonal staring first at her and then all about them in amazement. Julia was dumbstruck: the final wave never hit. Everything was calm. Leonal freed himself of the ropes and dashed over to Julia, gathering her in his arms.

"How can this be?" he asked her. "I thought I … I thought we'd lost you."

"The King!" announced Kai, his voice resounding in their minds. "The King has turned the tide! Tia and Fin, they did it! They got him to do it!"

Julia looked at Leonal, her eyes wide in disbelief. She was awestruck by the power her grandfather possessed. She had, of course, heard the stories about his ability to control the tide, but seeing it here and now was more than she could comprehend.

"Such power," was all she could say.

"Come on, let's see if those legs are still working," said Leonal, getting Julia to her feet.

Her knees were bleeding from hitting the deck but she did not seem to have sustained any further injuries and was able to walk to the railing of the ship without too much support from Leonal. He held her arm all the same. They looked out at the now calm seas, hardly believing that these were the same waters that had been about to consume them only moments before. Everyone but the captain made their way towards them, where they met at the rail.

"Maurice remains at the wheel," said Tresgar, "but it seems the King has come to our aid. The sea should present us with no further problems."

"You will feel the sands of home between your toes in no time at all, Julia," added Macki.

Julia heard them but did not take her eyes away from the water.

"No sign of our friends?" asked Tresgar, concern etched across his face.

"None," replied Julia in barely more than a whisper.

Leonal put his hand on hers.

"We were nearly all lost," he reminded her. "Pascal and the Grippon went into those waters willingly and saved us all. They are true heroes, both."

Finally, Julia turned away from the sea, for the others to see her crying.

"They did it for me," she said. "They're gone because of me. Those waves were too fierce for any creature to have survived. I shouldn't have let them. I shouldn't have—"

Suddenly, there was a mighty crashing sound, as a great torrent poured down upon the deck. There in the water, swimming alongside the boat, were two colossal figures.

"What a lovely day for a swim!" Pascal called out to them, smiling while he casually performed a perfect backstroke.

"Hi Julia!" shouted the Grippon. "I so worried about you. You okay?"

"Am I okay?" called Julia, her tears of grief turning to those of joy on seeing her dear friends safe. "Yes, I am okay, Grippon. But you two, I thought we had lost you. Those waves were so brutal."

"Told you we good swimmers," laughed the Grippon before disappearing under the water, springing out and crashing back in, soaking everyone in the process.

Julia stood alone, looking out across the crystal-blue waters. Pascal and the Grippon were quite content to swim the remainder of the journey, so strong were they in the water. The others had returned to Maurice to help make the ship ready for landing. Julia could now clearly see the golden sands of Hamunite before them. Their voyage was almost at an end and here was the land that her father had once known as home.

Her grandfather awaited her there; a man of such power that he could command these very seas and bend them to his will. Having now witnessed the King's power first hand, Julia could not comprehend the notion that she herself possessed the same ability. It simply did not seem possible to her. She was beginning to feel overwhelmed, when Macki interrupted her pondering.

"Beautiful, isn't it?" he said. "It doesn't matter how many times I make this voyage, I never grow tired of the sight of home."

"Home," said Julia quietly, as it dawned on her. "Do you know, Macki, I don't believe I've ever truly known a home. The place that I'd thought to be my home, the one in which I spent my childhood, was a prison all along without my knowledge. Martinez kept me and my mother there against our will. Can you call a place home, Macki, when you do not ever get to choose to leave?"

"Of that I am unsure," he replied, "but what I do know is that even if you didn't have a home before, you certainly do now, Your Highness."

"I may well get used to calling Hamunite home," she smiled, "but I don't think I am ever going to get used to people calling me Your Highness."

"Well, if Your Highness ever tires of leading the life of luxury," came a voice from behind them, making them turn around, "she will always be welcome to come and rough it on our farm," Leonal said laughing, as he and Mikel returned.

'"How dare you!" said Julia in mock astonishment.

"One thing I can tell you about this one," offered Mikel, "is that she is not afraid of hard work. For many years, I knew her a simple serving girl and in all that time she never once shied away from any task. We could not wish for a better future queen."

Julia thought she could see a tear in the dwarf's eye but this was quickly interrupted when the ship jerked again and another almighty splash rained down upon the deck, drenching them anew.

"All right, Grippon!" Macki shouted over his shoulder, after shaking off the latest deluge. "You've had your fun but some of us have already got wet enough for one day!"

"It's not the Grippon," said Leonal, looking beyond Macki and Julia, his eyes wide with terror.

"The serpent!" yelled Mikel.

Julia turned to look but was immediately dragged back from the railing by Macki. As he pulled her away from the edge, she saw the creature rising from the sea. Its enormity seemed submerged beneath the water, yet it wound up and up, until it loomed at least twenty feet into the air. It bore thousands of opaque, tight-knitted scales of amethyst and obsidian, and when it finally lifted its head, Julia saw a crown of dark-spiked horns, resembling a black sun against the blue sky. As she looked into its enormous eyes that flashed in the deep red of a raging fire, she feared they were the last things she would ever see.

Staring down at them, the serpent opened its mouth to make a horrifying, gurgled roar, then lashed its head towards them, bearing its terrifying, razored teeth. Before it could plough into the ship, the Grippon sprung from the water and clenched one of its spiny horns in its powerful jaws, pulling it back down to where Pascal was waiting. Together, they wrestled with the sea creature that dwarfed even them.

"Bondsmen, draw your arrows!" hollered Macki, as he began firing upon the serpent. Aaron joined him and from above them, on the captain's deck, Rob and Donald added to the onslaught. They shot relentlessly, but to their despair each and every arrow ricocheted off the sea beast's hard scales. Maurice appeared beside them with a heavy harpoon gun over his shoulder.

"If this doesn't take her down, nothing will!" yelled the captain. "Now, come to me, my beauty!"

He launched the harpoon. The beast let out a roar. For a brief moment, Maurice thought he had vanquished this most formidable of foes – until he saw his missile rebound and fall beneath the waters. Instead of hurting it, the harpoon had only enraged it. It flung Pascal with its head, before coiling its immense body around the Grippon and plunging into the water, taking it below. The companions looked on in horror, as Pascal dived down after them.

"The serpent is a creature of the sea of Hamunite," said Tresgar. "We need King Joalian to make it cease this onslaught or we are all done for!"

He turned his mind to the young hawkwing above them.

"Kai, speak to Tia and Fin. Tell them that the King needs to command the beast to stop. He needs to do it now, Kai!"

Kai relayed the message to his fellow hawkwings, which was received immediately. Tia and Fin gave each other a despairing look as the update came through, for King Joalian had remained unconscious since his great effort to calm the seas. Tia was not hopeful but she knew she needed to try and rouse the King all the same.

"Your Highness! King Joalian! Can you hear me?" she called with her mind, but the King did not shift. "Your Highness, please – we need you one more time. You have calmed the waves but a giant sea serpent has risen and is attacking our friends. We need you to command it to stop or it will surely destroy their ship and they will all be killed!"

For all of Tia's desperation, the old King remained motionless. Fin came over from his place at the window, where he had witnessed the serpent's attack. He went right up to Joalian's face and, to Tia's astonishment, he began trying to shake the King into consciousness.

"Fin, what are you doing?" she said aghast.

"He needs to wake up!" said Fin frantically. "They're all going to die if he doesn't wake up!"

Tia looked at Fin and then decided there was nothing for it but to join him. They knew how close their friends were to meeting their end. Together, they tried with all their strength to push and pull him into consciousness. But still he did not come round.

Fin ended his efforts and turned to Tia, dejected. All they had done had been for nothing.

"It's over," he said. "We've failed. Julia will never reach Hamunite to claim her birthright."

"Julia!" said Tia, her tear-filled eyes widening in realisation. "The King cannot help us, but his heir is right there on the ship. He is no longer strong enough to call upon the help of the gods for their power over the seas, but perhaps she is!"

"Yes," agreed Fin. "It might just work."

Tia turned her mind back out to sea and called out to Kai.

It had seemed an eternity to Julia since the sea serpent had disappeared back beneath the water. As she looked out for any sign of friend or foe, Kai's voice came into her head.

"Princess, how large has your birthmark become now?" he asked.

"I'm not sure," she replied. "I haven't thought to check it for some days now."

Julia reached her hand up to her neck and pulled it away in shock. Slowly, she moved her fingers back to feel the contours of her birthmark. She was astounded at how large it had become without her noticing. Almost double the size! She relayed this to Kai, who in turn informed her that he had a message for her from Tia.

Just then the ship lurched Julia knew this could mean only one thing. Waves lashed against the side of the vessel, as the horned crown of the serpent began to re-emerge from the deep. She stood paralysed. Its terrible eyes came back into view and were soon looking down on her once again.

"Julia!" called Kai. "Listen to me. Tia says that although you need your grandfather's teachings to control your powers safely, you may already have enough to ask for the gods' help. Your birthmark has grown, as you have got nearer to Hamunite. But not only your mark. Your powers – they have grown, too!"

"I can't imagine ever being able to calm the seas," replied Julia hesitantly, "let alone have any effect on a creature such as this!"

"You are stronger than you know," said the young hawkwing. "You can do this, Julia. You must. You are our final hope."

The serpent was now back towering above the ship, preparing to strike down and lay it to waste. There was no sign of Pascal or the Grippon.

"Very well," she said, gathering herself quickly. "What must I do?"

"Call to the gods, as you would to us hawkwings," he explained. "We are their creation, as is the sea serpent. Reach out with your mind and ask for their help to tame it."

"Okay," said Julia. "I will try."

She took one last look at the serpent, as it pulled its head back to attack, before she closed her eyes and spoke the words.

"I call upon the gods to free my friends from the sea serpent and allow us all safe passage to the harbour. I ask in the name of

Hamunite and King Joalian. In the name of my father, Jacob, I beg this of you!"

Julia opened her eyes and was startled to see the face of the sea serpent hovering mere yards away from her own. It looked at her long and searchingly before returning to the sea and, in a matter of moments, it disappeared from view completely. The ship began to rock less ferociously until it was soon gently lulling.

Donald shouted out in excitement from where he and Rob were still standing on the captain's deck.

"Look – there in the distance – coming out onto the beach!"

Two hulking figures were slowly crawling onto the sands of the cove. Shouts of joy erupted across the ship. Julia's heart had never in her life felt as grateful as it did now to see the courageous Pascal, and with him the unwaveringly brave Grippon, stumbling onto dry land, alive.

Maurice Mariner expertly brought the ship to rest at the harbour wall; his crew members jumped down and fastened the ropes securely. Lady Alessandra and Philippe returned from below and joined the others on deck.

"There you are, Tresgar," said Lady Alessandra. "It wasn't exactly a leisurely cruise down there, but I managed to keep your son safe enough, I think."

One after another the passengers made their way down the gangplank. As Julia took her first steps onto the land to which she was heir, she could not help but feel a little overwhelmed. She had been so occupied with just staying alive that she had not had the time to take in the enormity of what was to come. Here she was – all her life a mere servant girl, and now a princess expected to one day rule this land. As if reading her thoughts, Mikel sought to ease her mind.

"You are thinking, how can I possibly do this – that you are just a servant girl and are undeserving and unprepared for such power and prestige as comes with being the princess of such a great place – am I right?"

"Something like that," said Julia, turning to look at her dear and loyal friend.

"It is understandable that you would feel this way," he said. She saw the smile in his eyes. "But your fears are completely unfounded."

"Unfounded!" she gasped. "Mikel, look at this place! How many people live on an island this size? There must be thousands!"

"Tens of thousands," he said, still smiling.

"How am I supposed to handle being responsible for tens of thousands of people?" she asked, exasperated.

"The answer is in your question," Mikel said, taking Julia's hand in his. "You will be responsible for them. A less-deserving heir may have said, 'How am I supposed to rule tens of thousands of people?' – but not you. You do not desire to rule anyone. Instead, your first thought is for the safety and well-being of those in your care. It has always been this way. It is who you were born to be."

At these words, Julia instinctively lifted her hand to the mark on the back of her neck, in the shape of the island of Hamunite. On seeing this, Mikel spoke again.

"No, it is not your birthmark that I speak of. You are a daughter of kings, it is true, but this is not why I say you were born for the role that awaits you. Where we are born and who we are born to, be it to kings or farmhands, great warriors or circus performers, is decided by no more than a roll of the gods' dice. The truth of why you are the right one to rule this land is not in your blood – it is in your heart. All these years I have watched you grow, and never have you shown anything but the greatest kindness to those you meet – many of whom, I might add, have not been deserving of it. That was why I hoped we would one day get you here, because I believed your kindness was what the world needed. Since we have travelled this long and perilous journey, I have seen that not only are you kind but also that there is great courage in you. The combination of this bravery and kindness is why you have protested every time against us putting ourselves at risk. Your refusal to let us give our lives for you is exactly the reason why it has been worth doing just that. You are more than ready for this next challenge," he said finally.

Julia smiled back at Mikel, her heart bursting with gratitude at his reassuring words.

"Well," she said, "I will do my best not to let you down."

"You never could," he replied.

"You could never let any of us down, Julia," drawled a familiar voice from behind her.

Julia turned. The tears that had been welling now streamed down her face in rivers of overwhelming joy, at the sight of the Grippon limping towards her with Pascal at his side. She dashed towards them. She felt the Grippon wince, as she buried herself in its wet fur. Pascal stooped to envelop her in his massive arms.

"I thought we'd lost you," Julia said.

Looking closer, she could see a large, nasty-looking gash along one of the Grippon's rear legs.

"You're hurt," she said, full of concern for her friend.

"Only scratch," it assured her. "Be lot worse if it not for Pascal. That thing had me. Not letting me go. Pull me down under water. About to slice through me with big, sharp teeth when Pascal bash it over head. It get my leg but far worse if not for Pascal," it said, nestling its furry head under the giant's arm. "Grippon be two of a kind if not for Pascal!"

"It was but a momentary respite, though," explained Pascal. "Although I spared my friend here from being cleaved in two, I was not able to free him. And furthermore, I now had the serpent's attention myself. It was moving too fast beneath the water and before I could react, it had spiralled itself around me and I too was then at its mercy. I can only assume that it was wary of further unseen attacks from above. When it kept us coiled in its body below, we saw it snake its head back towards you."

"We try to fight and come help," promised the Grippon. "I bite down on it but Grippon's teeth not get through scales."

"We were weakening," added Pascal. "We had been below water too long and were losing the strength to fight. We were drowning."

"Thought we never see you again, Julia," said the Grippon, an enormous tear falling to the ground.

"But then the strangest thing happened," the giant added. "Just when we thought we had met our end, the serpent simply let us go. Not only that, we saw it swim away. We could not believe we were free. With the last breath in our bodies, we were able to swim up and break back through to the surface."

"That would be the work of our Princess," said Mikel, causing Julia's neck to flush.

"What you do, Julia?" asked the Grippon in amazement.

"I … I called upon the gods," said Julia, still not quite believing it herself. "I asked them to command the serpent to let you go and to allow us safe passage to the island."

The two oversized friends stood awestruck before Pascal finally spoke.

"You truly are the Princess of Hamunite," he said.

"That she is," Macki said, smiling, as he joined them along with the other members of their party. "Now, Your Highness, if you don't mind, I think it is time we went to meet your grandfather."

27

Homecoming

As they made their way towards the castle fortress, through the winding streets of Hamunite, the people came from their homes to marvel at this most curious of processions. Yet, the people were not afraid of this strange ensemble. They welcomed Macki and the Bondsmen as fellow Hamunites among the party and, while they were certainly shocked to see a giant walking their streets, not to mention the dog-like beast – which none of them had ever before seen anything of its like – they recognised something of themselves in the girl riding on its back.

"Macki, you old rascal!" called a voice. "You've kept some odd company in your time, but this is something altogether quite different, even for you!"

"You talk like you've never seen a Grippon before, my friend!" he hollered back.

"What in the blazes is a Grippon?" asked another onlooker.

"Something quite wonderful," replied Macki, with the deepest sincerity.

Just then, a child wriggled its way free from the crowd and stepped out towards them; a young girl of perhaps six or seven years of age. She came right up to the Grippon and stroked its fur with her small hand.

"Is your dog a Grippon then?" she asked Julia.

But, to the child's amazement, the beast answered her question itself.

"I not a dog," it said. "I am a Grippon. Well, not *a* Grippon, *the* Grippon. I one of a kind."

"You can talk!" said the child, astonished.

"I talk, little one," replied the Grippon. "Talk and climb and swim and look after Julia."

"That's me," said Julia, smiling down at the child. "And he certainly does all that and more."

"Wow!" was all the little girl could say, as the procession moved on towards the castle.

As they reached the castle gate, two Hamunite guards greeted them. They bowed low to Julia and Lady Alessandra before explaining that they had been expected.

"The hawkwings have told us of your coming, Your Highness, My Lady and all of our honoured guests. You are the talk of the castle," said the first guard.

"It is our great honour to welcome you to Hamunite," added the second, as they stepped aside and signalled to fellow guards stationed above to open the gate.

Another guard was awaiting them beyond the gate, to escort them to the main castle. They were led through lavish grounds. Julia saw plants and flowers she had never seen before, arrayed around pools in which children were bathing and playing. They followed a path that weaved its way through gardens filled with even more curious foliage. A group of hawkwings sat nestled in a nearby tree and bade Julia and her companions welcome.

They met more guards as they reached the main entrance to the castle and were again given a warm welcome as they were admitted. It was large enough for even Pascal and the Grippon to pass through without needing to lower their heads.

"Your Highness, My Lady," spoke the guard who had escorted them. "As you are no doubt aware, the King has not been in the greatest of health of late. Furthermore, his considerable efforts in aiding your passage across the sea have left him very weak and he is in need of rest. However, he has given us explicit instructions that you are not to be kept waiting, such is his desire to meet his granddaughter. That said, and with His Majesty's health in mind, as the head of his guard, may I perhaps suggest that just yourselves come to his chambers and that introductions to the rest of your party, whom he has heard all about from your hawkwing friends and has a great desire to meet, wait until a little later when his vigour is restored."

"Yes, of course," said Julia, before turning to her friends. "Do you think you will all be able to stay out of trouble for a short time while my grandmother and I meet my grandfather?"

"Us stay out of trouble?" teased Macki. "I don't know what you could mean. When have any of us, yourself included, had anything other than plain sailing?"

They all laughed heartily at this. Julia looked at each of them; she could scarcely believe that they had made it, after everything they had endured.

"Thank you, all of you," she said. "There is no doubt in my mind that I would not be here without your help and the sacrifices each of you has made."

"There is no doubt in my mind," replied Tresgar, "that to each of us you are worth it. Now go, Your Highness, King Joalian awaits you."

Julia and Lady Alessandra walked arm in arm, as the guard led them up a great stairway and along a passage to the ornately carved double doors to King Joalian's chambers.

"Are you ready, my dear?" asked Lady Alessandra.

"Yes," replied Julia. "I believe that I am."

The doors swung open to reveal a lavishly decorated room. There, propped up by a great number of pillows and cushions on a four poster bed that looked out onto the sea, sat a frail old man. Two hawkwing messengers hovered either side of him. Their attention turned to the newcomers in the room.

"Julia!" burst Tia's voice telepathically, as she sped through the air towards her. "Oh Julia, you were amazing. I knew you could do it. We couldn't wake King Joalian after he had calmed the seas but Fin and I, we knew that you had it in you to tame the serpent."

"The King is very much awake now," spoke King Joalian in a voice that, despite its frailty, still wrung with authority. "And he seeks your forgiveness for being unable to have seen you all the way across the sea – for that and for many other foolish mistakes he has made. Please, my dear ladies, would you come closer. It shames me to say I am confined to this bed for the time being."

Fin told them how pleased he was to see them well, before going to rest by the large window, where Tia joined him. As they came closer, Julia could see that the King looked thin and weary. The years had lined his face and his skin hung loose, where once it would have clung tight to muscle. It was Lady Alessandra to whom King Joalian first spoke.

"My Lady, your very presence brings light to this Kingdom. It is clear to me that while the ravages of time have done what they have to me, you clearly remain untouched by its cruelness. However, age and decrepitude are the least of what I deserve. I beg your forgiveness, My Lady, as I will beg the same of your daughter should the gods grant me enough time to meet her. My behaviour towards Isabella and to my very own son, Jacob…" he trembled, "…may well be unforgivable."

Tears formed in the King's eyes.

"Had I not banished my son, he and his new wife could have lived here happy and safe. It was the decision of one too reckless to look past his pride to what really matters – family."

His eyes fell upon Julia, as he said this last word.

"I lost my son forever because of a foolish feud started between two countries long before any of us were even born."

"My forgiveness will not bring your son back," said Lady Alessandra. "And neither can that of my daughter. However, even though it has been many years since I have been able to see Isabella, I have known through messages from the hawkwings that she lives. I do not know if I could have carried on had she suffered the same fate as your son. Losing a child is the worst thing any parent can ever go through and so to my mind, Joalian, you have paid the greatest price for your mistakes. It is time for us to move beyond our old world of disdain and fear between nations. A new world is upon us," she said, looking to Julia and then the King. "A better world, one in which old mistakes need to be learned from. And in that spirit, I do forgive you."

"Thank you, My Lady," he said, the tears now running freely down his cheeks, into his white beard. "I do not have the words to express my gratitude."

"Then do not try to find them. Your time will be better spent now getting to know Julia," said Lady Alessandra, as she moved away from the bed to join the hawkwings at the window.

King Joalian looked up from his bed at his granddaughter.

"Come here, child. Allow this old man to look upon you."

She stepped forward anxiously and he patted the side of the bed as an invitation for her to sit. She did so and there they sat, searching each other's faces.

"Hello, my dear," Joalian croaked with emotion. "You are no child at all, I see, but a beautiful young woman. What an absolute fool I have been to have missed your growing up and to have lost my son, all because of my own stupidity and failure to embrace others – which was the very purpose of the mission to which I had entrusted Jacob."

Julia was touched by the sincerity of his words, but also knew that this was not just about the meeting of an estranged family member. It was about something far bigger than them. The fate of thousands of people was in their hands.

"Although I never got to meet him, I feel that my father is a part of me. He will be with me always, as I believe he is with you. We will never forget him, Grandfather, but we must all look to the future now. We have friends who will do all they can to help us and Hamunite. President Olivia Ollisiro of Roscar has made a promise to commence treaties with Hamunite and to offer her services as mediator in any talks we may need to have with Jahimia."

"You called me 'Grandfather'," King Joalian responded, as if that was the only word he had heard. "Oh, what a wonderful chance I have been given. However long or short the time I have left, I promise to cherish every minute."

"Yes, Grandfather," said Julia. "This is very true, but the treaties—"

"Yes, of course. You are right," said the King. "President Ollisiro is an honourable woman and will be a welcome ally."

Julia was relieved to know that her words had not gone above the King's head.

"Now, we need to form a plan. I must meet with the rest of your party immediately, for there will be a role to play for all."

"The head of your guard told us that you will need time to rest before you meet the others," Julia protested.

"I have sat idly by for too long, my dear," he said, "and I fear that the time will soon be upon me when I shall rest forever. No, this is too important. Call the guards. I shall need to suffer the indignity of being carried to the throne room, but I refuse to let my pride come before what needs to be done – ever again."

The size of the throne room made Lady Alessandra's great hall look like a common living area by comparison, to the extent that even if the Grippon perched on Pascal's shoulders, it would still not be able to reach the vast ceiling, which was intricately painted to depict the years of history of the great nation of Hamunite. The companions made their way towards the thrones at its end. King Joalian sat on the regal throne and smiled at his visitors as they approached. Seated next to him, in a slightly smaller, but no less lavish, throne was Julia; and sat beside her, Lady Alessandra.

"Come forward, all of you," ordered the King.

The companions did as they were bid and King Joalian looked upon them all in turn with kind eyes.

"Macki, my good man," he said, delighted to see the roguish bondsman, "and your boy, Aaron, too – I owe you so much. That goes for you other Bondsmen, too," he said, looking to Donald and Rob, "and the rest of your number across the sea, I am sure."

"Our numbers are less than they were, Your Majesty," replied Macki, "but every fallen Bondsman would tell you that it was worth it to see Julia sat beside you, as we do now."

Julia wanted to say that she did not wish for anyone to have died for her to be there, but the words got trapped in her throat, as she tried to keep her emotions in check.

The King addressed the whole party. "You have all done my granddaughter, and therefore my country, a great service. I look forward to getting to know each of you and hearing your stories in great depth, however big they may be."

He made this last point with a warm smile directed at Pascal and the Grippon. "But for now, there is still much to do. Julia has made this very clear to me."

"That is one of her many gifts, Your Majesty," said Mikel.

"I am most looking forward to finding out all about them, my friend," said the King. "In the meantime, we have work to do. I have already messaged Tia, Fin and Kai and given a telepathic mission to each. I would ask of your sea captain to go to Great Holm and give passage to some very special visitors. Macki, I know that you have not yet had a chance to see your family, but I need to ask that you also make the voyage. The safety of these guests is paramount to negotiations beginning smoothly, and there is no other I trust with such a task than you."

"If Your Majesty would allow me to have this evening to spend with my Meggie, while Maurice readies the ship, then I am yours to command as always," was Macki's reply.

"Of course. I am learning all too well how valuable time with family is," said the King, with a look to Julia at his side. "If you take the young Jahimian boy with you when you sail, this should also show our intention to make a peaceful alliance."

On hearing this, Leonal's first thought was that he did not want to leave Julia. However, the King was putting great faith in him – and he would be glad of the chance to see his mother again. He looked at Julia and then the King and admitted as much before making his final declaration.

"It will be my honour to play my part in this mission, Your Majesty," he said.

"Grandfather, who are our special guests?" asked Julia.

"I am issuing an invitation, through the hawkwings, to King Jared, informing him that I wish to finally make the peace we failed to do many years ago. I am asking that he bring with him Isabella and President Ollisiro. If Leonal wishes to bring his mother back with him, she, too, will be most welcome."

Julia was overjoyed to hear this news and struggled to contain her happiness at the prospect of being reunited with her mother. Leonal, too, was thrilled that not only was he going to see *his* mother, but that he would be able to tell her that she was invited to Hamunite as the guest of its illustrious King.

"Now Macki, Aaron," said Joalian, "I know you are eager to get back to Meggie; however, before you head home, I must ask you all to join me outside while I address my people. As soon as the ship is ready, we shall start to build the new world, making it a better one for all."

"Grandmother," said Julia, turning to Lady Alessandra, "we're going to see Mamma!"

Lady Alessandra drew Julia into her arms and shared a smile with King Joalian.

On a beautifully carved throne, two guards conveyed King Joalian to a wooden veranda overlooking the mountain peak on which the castle fortress was built. Looking down, he saw that hundreds of the people of his Kingdom had already congregated below. It was apparent that word of the arrival of their strange visitors had brought people out of their homes. Eventually, they all came to rest on a grassy bank just below the veranda, with the King, Julia and her ensemble of companions looking out from above.

King Joalian signalled to one of the guards and was handed a cone-shaped instrument, which he used as a loudhailer.

"People of Hamunite, it is with immense gladness that I can tell you that we have a princess – an heir, who can turn the tide!"

The crowd were in raptures.

"Unbeknown to me, before his death, my son, Jacob, and his wife, Isabella, had been expecting a child. That child is now a grown woman and she has returned to us."

He held his hand out to Julia, who stepped forward to take it. "I give you Princess Julia!" he hailed.

The crowd cheered even louder and Julia made out shouts of *Welcome home, Princess Julia!* and *Thank the gods for you, Princess Julia!*

The King spoke on. "She and her loyal companions are to be treated with great respect. Welcome, friends, companions of Princess Julia. You are most welcome here on Hamunite. Whether that be for a short stay or to settle here, we would be honoured if you chose to make Hamunite your home."

"Welcome to Hamunite!" the people praised.

"To the people of Hamunite," the King went on, "relay this news to all fellow countrymen and spread this message: HAMUNITE HAS A FUTURE!"

"HAMUNITE HAS A FUTURE!" echoed the crowd.

"Lastly, I tell you this," said the King, once the cheers had died down. "Soon, we will have more visitors – important visitors from the lands of Jahimia and Roscar. Welcome them as you have these wonderful friends of ours. Together, we shall build a better world!"

As the King and his party made their way from the veranda, they could hear the shouting and merriment rippling on across the land.

"You hear it, Pascal? We be invited to live here."

"I heard, Grippon, I heard. We will have much to do to find a suitable spot in which we can settle down without causing problems for the inhabitants, but it is a very good feeling to be welcomed as we have. I am feeling very positive about life on Hamunite."

The group began to break up to go their separate ways. Julia, with Leonal at her side, managed to speak with Aaron before he caught up with his father.

"Aaron, I am very curious," Julia said. "Who is Meggie?"

"All this time together and yet there is still so much to tell you all," said Aaron. "Meggie is my little sister. From time to time, we so-called Bondsmen make our way home to Hamunite by messaging the hawkwings to arrange our safe passage. My mother and I were left here when Father accompanied Jacob to Jahimia on his mission. They were best friends. They grew up together, learning the skills of archery, swordsmanship and how to protect Hamunite, as is every man's duty on this land. My mother, Susan, gave birth to Meggie some five years ago. It was not an easy birth and Mother took a turn for the worse. She passed away shortly afterwards. My father arrived soon after being messaged, too late to say goodbye to her. However, I was still living here at that time. My Aunt Rose and I sat by her side until her last breath. When Father came home, he decided to take me with him. I was fourteen years old and Aunt Rose and my father's brother, my Uncle James, agreed to bring up Meggie as they have no children of their own. She has been an absolute joy to them both, as indeed she is to Father and me."

"It seems to me, my friend, that we three have all suffered the loss of a dear parent because of the ongoing disputes between Hamunite and Jahimia," Leonal sympathised.

"Well, my loyal friends, I will make it my life's work to end all animosity between our countries. Aaron, I can't wait to meet Meggie," Julia enthused. "I think we should now all get some rest. Grandmother and I are being given rooms in Grandfather's living quarters. Hawkwings are going to lead Grippon and Pascal to their settlement. Fin has messaged them to say that he thinks there is a suitable resting place nearby. Aaron, you need to get Macki and get going to your home and your family."

"Indeed, Your Highness. I look forward to the time when I can next serve you," said Aaron, as he made his way to catch up to Macki.

Suddenly, it occurred to Julia and Leonal that they were in a position that until now had proved to be extremely rare – they were alone together. They stood halfway between the veranda and the castle entrance in an awkward silence, neither of them, it seemed, able to find any form of language to aid them.

"Be careful back on the sea, won't you?" Julia eventually managed to say.

"I will," Leonal promised. "Though, it will sadden me greatly to part from you."

Julia felt the warmth rush to her cheeks at his words but managed to compose herself.

"You will be back here soon enough, I am sure," she said.

"One hundred sea serpents couldn't keep me away," joked Leonal.

"I think I will have to look into the business of breeding sea serpents so that we might find out."

Mikel's voice startled them, as they span round to face him.

"Either that or an army of dwarves to keep an eye on you, boy," he added with a smile.

"I already can't take a step without one of you spying on me," said Leonal, though there was no trace of anger in his voice. "I despair to think how it would be with an army of you!"

"Mikel, we were just talking," protested Julia.

"I am well travelled, my young friends," Mikel said, fixing them a mock stare. "I know where just talking gets young people."

This caused them both to blush.

"Now, come on, the pair of you, back into the castle. Your absence has not gone unnoticed by those of us old enough to know better."

28

Coming Together

The next morning, down at the harbour wall, Maurice Mariner and his crew prepared their ship to sail back to Great Holm. Gathered on the embankment were the rest of the companions, along with Julia, Lady Alessandra and Macki's family. Meggie shyly held onto her aunt's hand, as she was introduced to Julia and the others.

"Are you really our Princess?" she asked Julia.

"Well, yes, it seems I am," Julia replied.

"Oh, it's like a fairytale!" Meggie smiled back delightedly.

"I know, that's how it seems to me, even though I have been living this very strange story. Do you know, your daddy and your brother and all our friends here are the real-life heroes of this story. You should be very proud of them all," Julia told her.

Rose then spoke to Julia.

"We can't thank you enough for coming home to us Hamunites and for our family. It means so much having Macki and Aaron back to live and work with us again. We have missed them so much."

Aaron stepped forward, to put his arms around his aunt and hug her. With a slight tremble in his voice, he said, "And we have missed you all, too. It will be good to sleep at night without having to stand guard. To live a life of farming and family seems like all our dreams come true."

"Okay," said Macki, "let's get this mission accomplished and then we can get back to living our dream."

After all the goodbyes had been said, Macki and Leonal joined Maurice and his crew on the journey back to Jahimia and Great Holm, with the promise of a swift return. Tresgar and Philippe were also joining the voyage and returning home to Roscar.

The trio of hawkwings had already set off south at the break of dawn; Kai to deliver the King's message to Olivia Ollisiro, and Tia and Fin to King Jared's castle, to message Isabella and the King himself. All had invitations for safe passage to Hamunite in order to discuss a treaty of mutual benefit between the countries.

The ship crossed the sea without incident and now, as they docked at Great Holm, the hawkwings messaged Macki to inform him that the guests would be at the harbour at noon the next day, ready to sail back with them to Hamunite.

"Right," Macki said, "we have a good few hours this evening to spare. I propose that we all go and pay our respects to Leonal's mother, and then Tresgar and Philippe can make their way home from there."

Leonal was eager to see his mother and, as an old family friend, Tresgar was also glad of an opportunity to check up on Maria and make sure she was well.

Maria was delighted to see them all, but, of course, Leonal especially, who quickly became embarrassed by all her hugging and kissing. Tresgar explained all that had happened and she hugged him even tighter.

"I'm your mother – it's allowed!" she protested. "I have missed you like crazy. Imagine if I had known the adventure you've been on. The worry alone would have given me a heart attack!"

"Mother, you can see I am fine. Now, are you going to take up the King's invitation and come to Hamunite with us?" Leonal asked.

"Try and stop me. I can't wait to meet the princess who has captured all your hearts. I just need to tell my friend Jessica to watch over my cottage and that she can take on my work for the next few days if she wants to."

They ate dinner together and shared more stories but soon enough it was time for Tresgar and Philippe to say their goodbyes. The friends embraced, with promises to meet again soon. As twilight descended, the father and son made the short journey to their own home. With a big day ahead of them, the others turned in for the night. Leonal gave up his bed for Macki and slept on a camp bed they kept for when they had visitors.

Morning came around quickly and Macki, Leonal and Maria were soon on their way to Great Holm in anticipation of the journey back to Hamunite. At noon, the people of Great Holm came together to see the strange ensemble of their King and his daughter Jasmina, along with Isabella and the President of Roscar, who had brought Vallis Vallier with her. Macki, Leonal and Maria boarded the large sailing ship together. There was much chatter, excitement and speculation among the common folk at what the purpose of this voyage was. Guardsmen patrolled the harbour area, quietly warning anyone who was being too outspoken or unruly to calm down and behave themselves.

As the ship sailed out of the harbour for Hamunite, a great cheer from the crowd echoed out onto the sea breeze, though no one knew quite what it was they were cheering for. Macki messaged the hawkwings, who were flying above the ship.

"Are you ready to message King Joalian to turn the tide, Tia?"

"Yes, indeed Macki. I will message him as soon as we are in sight of the cove," Tia answered.

Having done this trip once already, Maurice was prepared for the pull of the tide and waited patiently for it to be turned before issuing commands to the crew to fully unfurl all three sails, to take in the winds blowing at a good rate behind them.

On the harbour wall, Julia and the King eagerly awaited the arrival, along with the remaining companions and the Royal Guard. King Joalian's strength was gradually returning and, with Julia holding his arm, he was now able to stand. A guard of honour had been arranged by the landing bridge, ready to receive the visitors.

Macki came first, escorting Olivia and Vallis, followed by Leonal with King Jared, Jasmina, Maria and Isabella. Julia cried on seeing her mother, and Leonal holding Isabella's arm in such a protective manner filled her heart with joy.

King Joalian himself stepped forward to greet his guests, shaking their hands and thanking them for agreeing to make this journey. Julia and Lady Alessandra embraced Isabella and all three generations cried in their reunion. Then, Julia spontaneously hugged Maria and Leonal, much to Leonal's delight.

Everyone was then guided up the hill to the castle, where the King's devoted servants had prepared a beautifully decorated space with a comfortably cushioned table and chairs at its centre. Once everyone was seated and had been offered refreshments, King Joalian began the proceedings.

"Thank you all for being here today at such short notice, my most esteemed and important guests. Isabella, I must beg your forgiveness. My rash judgement all those years ago cost me my son, you your husband and Julia her father."

King Jared interrupted.

"I, too, beg forgiveness from Isabella and Julia – and from you yourself, King Joalian. As unbelievable as it seems, I had no idea what Martinez had been up to, or of the atrocities he had carried out. The man's bigotry is truly outrageous, although I understand his treatment of your family is more to do with greed. His own father had passed down stories of the gold caves of the former Jahamunite which, of course, are now a part of only Hamunite."

"Indeed they are," answered King Joalian. "In fact, they form part of the hawkwing settlement. You have had the honour of meeting Tia, Fin and Kai, I understand. The hawkwings are an integral part of what this country of Hamunite is all about."

"I find them fascinating and wonderfully intelligent advisers, Your Majesty," offered Olivia.

"Yes, indeed, President," said King Joalian. "And from what Macki has told me, I feel you and Roscar would be superb allies of Hamunite. Indeed, this is the main reason for my inviting you all here. I am determined that the time has come for the animosity of our forefathers to end. Hamunite's population has dwindled and many of our young men have passed through both of your countries in the hope of finding wives and having families of their own. Macki and his men were only ever there to offer them support and safe passage. If he agrees, I should like to offer Macki the post of Ambassador of Hamunite. He would relay any developments we, as countries, might need to share in the future. However, Macki may feel he has spent enough time away from his home and family."

"That is quite so, Majesty. I will need to discuss this idea at some length with my family," Macki answered, looking a little uncomfortable at this news.

"Yes, my good man," said Joalian. "We may continue this discussion privately, if you wish."

Dialogue on how the three countries could best work to make alliances worthwhile lasted the day. King Jared also revealed that General Martinez was no longer a general at all but a prisoner, along with Simeon, in the castle dungeons. A new General of the Guard had been appointed. Julia asked what had become of Marco and his mother and was informed that they had been rehoused in servants' quarters within the castle.

As evening descended upon them, King Joalian extended his

invitation to his guests to stay overnight, with a promise of a tour of the island the next day.

After a good few hours of revelling, King Joalian called them all together.

"Honoured guests and friends, please forgive me but I must say goodnight to you all. Though it saddens me to do so, I tire easily these days. Thank you all for coming here today on what I am sure will be remembered a historic day for our great nations. Please enjoy yourselves and I shall look forward to seeing you all for breakfast in the morning."

Macki spent most of the evening engaged in conversation with Olivia Ollisiro, who made it very clear that should he take on the role of Ambassador of Hamunite, he would be most welcome in Roscar. Macki tried to explain that he needed to spend time with his son and daughter as a family, to which Olivia responded by saying that he could bring them with him. He promised to let her know his decision once he had spoken with his family and the King.

As the evening wore on, fatigue got the better of all the guests and they gradually dispersed in search of their beds. Pascal and the Grippon made their way to the hawkwing settlement and returned to the place they had been shown the previous night. Their new home was ideal; a large cave that was big enough for them both to lie down in and hidden by overhanging willow trees. Nearby was a freshwater lake from which the hawkwings got their drinking water. It was perfect for them and reminded them of their home in the mountains.

The others had all been given quarters in the fortress, including Leonal and Maria, who had spent most of the evening in the company of Julia, Isabella and Lady Alessandra. Once they had all retired to their rooms, Isabella, who was sharing with Julia, pulled her daughter into a hug.

"Oh, my darling, I love your friends! I can't believe how well everything has turned out. Speaking of friends, though, I think young Leonal likes you as rather more than that."

"Mamma, please stop!" Julia blushed.

"Okay, I will stop."

"He is so handsome, though, my darling," she added.

They went to bed facing each other, just as they had on that night when Isabella had told Julia the truth about her heritage, but neither found that sleep came easily. So much had happened in such a short time. Isabella thought of how proud Jacob would have been of all that their daughter had accomplished and what a fine young woman she was becoming. Finally, sleep did come and in no time at all the sun was rising upon a new day.

Come the morning everyone convened for breakfast. Once they had eaten, King Joalian called them out onto the veranda overlooking the town and harbour to greet the smallfolk. Outside the fortress walls, Hamunites from all over the country had come together to see the new princess and her strange companions for themselves, after news of them had spread throughout the land.

Using his loudhailer, King Joalian introduced the party individually. Loud cheers of welcome resounded all around; the loudest for Macki and Aaron, who were recognised by the people as their own countrymen. This was until Julia came forward, when the crowd erupted into euphoria for their future queen.

On returning to the castle, Isabella, Lady Alessandra and King Joalian found time to discuss their futures. Isabella decided she would like to split her time between staying with her mother in Triorey, on Jahimia, and here on Hamunite with her daughter, Julia.

"They are my family and I need to make sure they are both well cared for," she said to the King. "Julia is here with her friends and now has you, her grandfather. I am sure she will always have someone looking out for her, but my mother is running a rather large estate by herself."

"Well, my darling, not quite by myself," said Lady Alessandra. "There are some loyal farming families who have stuck by me throughout the years. Nevertheless, ensuring that the people of Triorey are kept safe and well provided for is no small undertaking and does not get any easier as the years pass. It would be wonderful to have family of my own there with me once again. However, Julia's future is what matters most and I do not wish for you to tear yourself away from your daughter for the sake of your mother."

"My Ladies, Julia will be well looked after and protected here," King Joalian promised. "As well as her very own loyal companions, most of whom I think may choose to make their homes here, she will have my own guard and the people of

Hamunite themselves to watch over her and see that she has everything she could possibly need."

"That is so very reassuring to hear, Your Majesty," said Isabella. "Yes, I am quite sure that I will not be away from my mother or daughter quite long enough for either of them to miss me too much."

At noon, the two Kings and the President of Roscar met to sign a peace treaty between their countries and arrange trade agreements. Each agreed to end all hostilities and from that day forth to work together to positively promote friendship between the great nations of Jahimia, Hamunite and Roscar.

It was decided that should either King Jared or President Ollisiro need to visit Hamunite, they would make contact with the Ambassador, who King Joalian was confident would be Macki, although this was still to be confirmed. Olivia made a point of letting Joalian know that she very much hoped that he was correct in his assumption.

King Joalian also explained that should any of them need to communicate in a more immediate sense, all they need do was think of the hawkwings. As long as the reason for messaging them was for the good of Hamunite, they would be able to pick up their thought waves and communicate telepathically.

By late afternoon Maurice Mariner was issuing orders to his crew in preparation for sailing back to Jahimia and Roscar. With the late afternoon sun glistening upon the sea, King Jared and his daughter, Jasmina, boarded the ship along with Olivia and Vallis. Maria and Lady Alessandra hugged their children on the harbour wall, with promises to return soon for a lengthier stay on Hamunite. King Joalian embraced them both and assured them that they would always be welcome. Mikel was also returning to Jahimia with them and had promised Julia that he would return once he had seen his parents and made sure they were safe and well, and had escorted Lady Alessandra and Maria back to their homes.

The Grippon, Pascal and Leonal were all staying on Hamunite, as were Macki and Aaron for the time being, though a date had been set for an official meeting with the King to formally arrange Macki's return to Roscar as Ambassador. He had agreed privately with King Joalian that he would take up the post and that Aaron and Meggie would join him when he travelled to Roscar to make his new home.

After the farewells were completed, the ship cast off. Everyone aboard promised to return for a special ceremony of thanks, in which they would celebrate the future of Hamunite and its new alliances with Jahimia and Roscar.

29

The Future

Julia could scarcely believe that an entire month had passed since Lady Alessandra, Mikel and the others had sailed away. It was not that she hadn't missed them – far from it – but she had been kept so busy since taking up residence on Hamunite that the time had simply whistled by. She spent many hours each day in the company of the King learning the history of Hamunite, the duties of its royal family to the people and, of course, learning the skills needed to control her inherited powers to turn the tide of the unforgiving seas that surrounded them.

As well as learning from her grandfather, Julia had decided that it was vital that she get to know the people of Hamunite and, in turn, for them to get to know her. Each day she would ride out, accompanied by varying companions but almost always by Leonal, to the many towns, villages and hamlets that made up the island nation. She particularly took great pleasure in her visits to the hawkwing settlement, for this was a place of great wonder and magic to her. There she visited Tia, Fin and Kai and was also introduced to the Grand Hawkwing himself, who was responsible for overseeing the safety of the entire hawkwing community. Visits to the settlement also meant the opportunity to see Pascal and the Grippon in their new surroundings. It brought Julia great delight to see how happy they were and how readily the people of Hamunite had accepted them.

She was lying on her bed in her chambers, taking a well-earned rest and pondering all she had seen and learned since she had been on Hamunite, when Tia's voice came into her head.

"Princess Julia, the ship has arrived safely in the harbour," the hawkwing informed her.

"Thank you, Tia," Julia responded telepathically. "Let the King know that I will be along to escort him to the celebrations shortly."

Now that the day for the celebration had arrived, every single inhabitant of Hamunite – man, woman and child – had made the pilgrimage across the island to a sacred clearing a short way from the hawkwing settlement. Great big boulders that had been placed there some time long ago, beyond living memory, created a circular arena. Facing out to sea was a sturdy stage constructed of planks of wood hewn from huge trees. Tens of thousands of Hamunites sat themselves on the steps that had been carved into the boulders and eagerly awaited the beginning of the ceremony.

Maurice had once again brought the guests from Jahimia and Roscar. This time, however, he, too, was a guest. He was to be recognised for his valiant voyage that had brought the Princess of Hamunite home. The guests met with King Joalian and Princess Julia at the castle and, together, they were led in procession to the arena, where they took their seats at the front of the stage.

King Joalian nodded to the head of his guard for the proceedings to start, whereupon a band of musicians opened the ceremony with some rousing music which finished with horns that sent a quiver of anticipation throughout the crowd. The King reached for his loudhailer.

"People of Hamunite, our honoured guests – I bid you welcome. You have been invited here today to meet your future queen. I know for certain that the story of how my granddaughter, Princess Julia, arrived here has been shared far and wide – and, I am sure – discussed at length between you all. In getting her here, we have some very special people to thank.

"Grand Hawkwing, has agreed with me that these people should be recognised, to show our unfaltering gratitude for all they have done. Therefore, we have decided that they shall each be awarded a golden hawkwing clasp to signify the great service, above and beyond the call of duty, which they have given to our country. Firstly, may I call upon Princess Julia herself to come forward?"

A resounding roar reverberated around the arena, as Julia came to stand before the King. It was clear that the people of Hamunite had already taken her to their hearts. King Joalian took the first clasp from the Grand Hawkwing and fastened it to Julia's cloak. She bowed before the King and upon rising, he whispered into her ear.

"You are more than I could have ever deserved," he said softly, "but you are everything that Hamunite deserves. Are you ready to speak to your people?"

Her heart was pounding to be stood before so many people, but taking the loudhailer from her grandfather, Julia began her address.

"I do not have the words to express to the people of Hamunite how grateful I am for the warm welcome you have given me. There were times, I must admit, when I was not sure I would ever make it here, so to stand before you now brings such great joy to my heart. I only hope I can serve you as well as you deserve."

The people chanted Julia's name.

"I have no doubt in my mind that I would not be here with you now had it not been for the bravery of my dear friends that sit on this stage with me today. It is my great honour to place the golden hawkwing clasps upon them, which have been so valiantly earned."

One by one the companions were called up to collect their clasps. Macki, Aaron, Leonal, Mikel and Pascal all came forward to receive the country's emblem of thanks; Pascal crouching as low as he could so that Julia was able to fasten his onto him. For the Grippon, the King had had a special scarf woven, on which its clasp would fit. Julia stroked its fur after tying the scarf about its neck.

"Thanks, Julia," it said. "This best day of my life."

"Mine too, Grippon," she smiled.

Tresgar, Philippe and Maurice collected their clasps along with Donald and Rob. Daniel and Lucia De Silva received theirs for the great care and kindness they showed to Julia and her companions, not to mention their bravery and resolve when it had come to dealing with Simeon.

"Let us not forget our wonderful hawkwings Tia, Fin and Kai," announced the King, "for showing the courage and intuition that truly makes Hamunite great."

The hawkwings fluttered forward.

Grand Hawkwing spoke telepathically into the minds of all in the arena.

"As you all know, we hawkwings exist to keep this land safe and free from outside influences. However, from time to time we need to communicate with the outside world. In this case, people from across three nations have come together to support one another, and I thank each and every one of them."

He now turned to face the three hawkwings.

"Tia and Fin are renowned members of the hawkwing community and no one can ever have been in any doubt that they would not let us down. Young Kai here was perhaps not so well known, but now he has flown further from home than any hawkwing has ever done before. Well done all of you. We, the hawkwing community, are so very proud of you all."

Cheers of *Hooray for the hawkwings!* echoed around the arena. King Joalian announced that there was to be a feast for all at the edge of the forest of Hamunite Town.

Finally, Julia spoke, her voice ringing true for all to hear.

"People of Hamunite, I want to thank you once more for the great love and kindness that you have shown to me and my friends. As the daughter of a Prince of Hamunite, this country is in my blood. However, I am also the daughter of a Lady of Jahimia, the country in which I was raised. Therefore, I do not wish to be recognised as either Jahimian or Hamunite. But, in the spirit of reconciliation between these great nations, from this day forth I am … Jahamunite! May the gods looking down upon us hear my words and bless us all."

The horns trumpeted and rapturous applause broke out again, this time gathering ecstatic and explosive momentum.

The feast was of a scale that the country of Hamunite had never before seen. Royalty and common folk sat side by side to share in the joy of the dawn of a new era.

Macki and Olivia gravitated towards each other. When he told her that he had agreed to become the Ambassador of Hamunite and that he and his children would be returning with her to Roscar, she wound her arms around his neck and pulled him towards her, kissing him full on the lips.

"I trust you approve of my decision, President?" Macki laughed.

"Most certainly," she answered with a wide smile.

Leonal and Julia, enthralled by all that had happened, stood just away from the crowd, examining their hawkwing clasps. Having spent so much time together since they arrived on Hamunite, they had grown closer than ever. This day had been no different.

"I think we should probably spend some time with our mothers and our other companions," Julia said, smiling at him.

"I know you're right," Leonal answered, "though I must admit that I very much enjoy the occasions when I get you all to myself."

At this response, Julia stood on tiptoes and kissed his cheek.

"Okay, I will agree…" Leonal said, "…if you do that to my other cheek."

Julia swapped sides and as she leaned in, he quickly turned his head towards her, kissing her lips as she did so.

King Joalian and Isabella had been watching the two young lovers from a nearby table. They now both began to laugh.

"The future is bright indeed!" beamed the King.

About the author

M A O'keefe is Coventry born and bred. She is a stroke survivor who, until early retirement in 2020, had worked in primary schools for 33 years as a teaching assistant. She loves to read and write, and becoming an author has been a dream of hers for quite sometime.

She also loves spending time with her family and friends. The phrase *'life is most definitely for living!'* is a motto she strongly believes in, and is thankful every day that she is able to follow her passion and write stories such as this.

Mandy is currently working on a sequel to this story and has other ideas for characters featured in this novel.

Acknowledgements

I'd like to thank Alexa Whitten at the Book Refinery for her guidance, and Yasmin Yarwood for her editing diligence. I would never have made it without them.

And my family and friends, who have helped me through my stroke recovery.